A RIVETING SIX-PART ADVENTURE

PART 5
WITHOUT THE DAWN

AND DEMONS WALK

ROGER
ELWOOD

BARBOUR
PUBLISHING, INC.
Uhrichsville, Ohio

Published by Barbour Publishing, Inc.
P.O. Box 719
Uhrichsville, Ohio 44683
http://www.barbourbooks.com

ecpa Member of the
Evangelical Christian
Publishers Association

Printed in the United States of America.

CHAPTER 1

Early on, during the summer of 1997, Clarice and Sarah Fothergill had been able to reach their parents and were regularly brought up to date regarding their mother's condition, which seemed to have stabilized, bringing some hope that her long slide was over, and she might live far longer than anyone had anticipated.

But hints of brewing danger were surfacing throughout Europe. Their father warned that they must be prepared to leave Switzerland much sooner than originally planned.

Clarice and Sarah were able to pick up hints via the Internet, a growing sinister aura that was as frightening as it was intangible. Yet they remained unconvinced of anything but the paranoia even of their father Cyril Fothergill, whose nerves had been on edge ever since his return from those extraordinary encounters during his odyssey of years before.

Then something changed.

Communication became ever more erratic. Sarah had her encounter in that nearby village. And it was increasingly difficult to get through to their parents.

To a greater extent, life in that valley was cut off from much of the rest of the world. That had always been its primary attraction. They could be monks of a sort but without the rigors of monastery life. A way of life unknown to billions of people across the planet was theirs, calm and fortifying, the true essence of what "vacation" should be all about.

Eventually—

Phone communication broke down completely. And no one had a shortwave radio in the valley.

Only their portable computer was left to provide a possible means of contacting Cyril and Elizabeth Fothergill.

But then that did not give them what they wanted.

For some reason, they could transmit but could not receive, at least from the British Isles, and suspected that Harold Edling had established martial law, giving him the power to control all communication, a necessary move to cut down on possible saboteur actions within Great Britain, saboteurs receiving their instructions clandestinely from command centers in the Middle East. Electronic mail could be sent, yes, but the messages were regularly intercepted and squelched.

However, isolated messages came through from other countries, including Australia, Uganda, and Turkey. And the two sisters got a panoramic view of what was going on in the world beyond that little valley.

The threat of global epidemic, thought to be a hoax at one time, turned out to be only part of a scheme to catch world governments off-guard, and lull them into complacency.

It worked.

The Muslims and, only recently implicated on an official basis, the newly resurgent Druids were, it seemed, becoming astonishingly successful with their alliance, spreading disease as well as bigotry, with Jews all over the world but particularly in Europe being victimized to such an extent that eerie reminders of the Holocaust were hardly uncommon.

Yet a growing minority began to wonder if there were more to it than just the combined efforts of two groups of anti-Christian, anti-Jewish, antiwestern world fanatics. Muslim leaders from a dozen countries continued to disavow any involvement in the worldwide epidemic of the hantavirus, and asked for cooperation in tracking down the real culprits. Could be it a resurgent neo-Nazi movement? Or a group similar to the Heaven's Gate cult but with the opposite obsession, not that of killing themselves and leaving the world behind, but killing the world and leaving themselves behind? Responsible Muslims were pleading for attention, and pointing out that their own people were now among the victims of the virus.

The problem was that no one was listening to them, world leaders given over to a kind of mob hysteria, equating the Muslim appeal with the treacherous actions of the Japanese ambassadors just prior to the bombing of Pearl Harbor.

In the meantime, millions of people fell victim to the onslaught of disease.

Dictators found that absolute power meant absolutely nothing in such times, for though they could control the lives of those living in subjection to them, they could do nothing about invisible germs bringing on the most painful of deaths.

The mysterious gang of evil perpetrators responsible was sending diseased rats everywhere. But not only these long-feared rodents were used as carriers. Even more insidious was the secondary means of spreading the hanta virus.

In an astonishing Machiavellianlike maneuver, one that initially seemed stupid to any outsiders who stumbled upon it, these masterminds bought control of a mustard company headquartered in the United States!

It apparently had been carefully chosen for its contracts with several domestic, as well as one international, airline catering services. Disease cultures were placed in mustard packets aboard thousands of air flights traveling everywhere in the civilized world....

Two thousand feet straight up.

A gray-stone monastery with no architectural flourishes to lessen its dreary appearance, the building could have been mistaken for a prison except that there were no bars in the windows, and confinement was voluntary.

It rested on an exceptionally large, flat ledge of solid rock jutting out from the side of the mountain located at the western end of the little valley, its simply designed but massive hand-chiseled form remaining largely hidden from view by anyone who happened to be looking up in that direction from below, set back as it was, a deliberate precaution arrived at by the original builders. These unheralded men of great proficiency were guided by a specific Vatican edict ensuring the privacy of those monks who were dedicated to a concept of Christian service founded solely on the principle of withdrawing from those contaminating influences that were endemic to the outside world.

At first, the size of the building surprised both sisters.

So large, Clarice exclaimed to herself, as her eyes took it all in, *and yet nothing can be seen from below.*

She had expected little more than a serviceable building about a third or less of its size, but, in fact, the monastery seemed every bit spacious enough to house at least three times the number of monks who were presently doing service there.

A short while later she learned that the men themselves were not the reason for its uncommon expanse.

Documents and relics by the hundreds were housed there.

"So many!" she exclaimed as she surveyed those that had been placed in just one room out of half a dozen reserved for the purpose of storage, not as living quarters, but then she and Sarah were taken to the other rooms, larger than that first one, the odor of musty age common to each one.

Scrolls.

Pile after pile, shelf after shelf.

Many of the scrolls dated as far back as the first-century church and some were suspected to be older than that.

Some were remarkably intact, some in bits and pieces, and needing to be handled in the most cautious manner.

In addition, leather-bound, handwritten journals took up space in each room, scores of these, and the monks who were working on them, studying, copying, dusting them off, regarded virtually each one with an almost worshipful reverence.

"Some go back as far as the time of Christ, journals and the scrolls and, regrettably, fragments in many instances," a rotund and well-versed monk named Brother Thaddeus Palmisano explained with great patience to Clarice and Sarah.

Clarice was rather puzzled.

"But I thought the Vatican itself, what with its army of guards and cardinals, would have been the more appropriate repository for such precious finds. One would assume that security concerns could have been addressed so much better in the center of Rome than out here!"

The monk's expression changed.

"There are reasons. . ." he said cryptically.

"Can you tell us?" Clarice persisted, ever curious.

Brother Thaddeus seemed faintly conspiratorial.

"Your assumptions about the Vatican are logical enough, but remember, where there are many, many people, and, indeed, people who have some knowledge about what is hidden in the catacombs, there is also a great potential for theft."

The monk spoke grudgingly, finding it hard to admit that the church was so vulnerable, efforts to keep the ancient items secure hampered by the lingering but antiquated assumption that surely no one would *dare* to steal anything right out from under the nose of Pope Adolfo.

After grumbling comically to himself—at least Clarice and Sarah thought he was being funny, though Brother Thaddeus would have disagreed with them if he had known their reaction—he told them something that seemed close to sacrilege, given his view of the place of the Catholic Church in the world.

"There have been any number of thefts during the past few years," he said with great difficulty. "Can you grasp that?"

Brother Thaddeus was clearly nonplused as he added, his bulk shaking, "What is the world coming to?"

Cyril Fothergill had told his daughters about the supposedly secure vaults beneath St. Peter's Basilica where the most treasured items were kept.

"From the catacombs?" Clarice asked. "People are

stealing from there? Have they no fear of being caught, of earning the displeasure of God Himself?"

For Sarah, there was another consideration.

"But what could people do with such parchments?" she pointed out. "Clearly these could not be sold. Who would buy them?"

Brother Thaddeus had an answer.

"If each represents a link with the past, then its theft represents a lessening of that link. If each contains some wisdom from those closest to Christ or their immediate successors, then the impact of the loss of that wisdom is incalculable."

"But what about the copies that exist?" Clarice asked. "The record would be preserved in those, would it not?"

"But not everything has been copied thus far," Brother Thaddeus explained. "And we have talked only about the *documents* as such. What about the relics? The bones of St. Peter, for example? The shroud that was used to cover Christ while He was in the tomb? And many, many more. No copies can be made of these. When they are lost, that is it, they are gone forever."

But Sarah was clearly troubled.

"Holy things. . .precious things. . ." she muttered. "They are not to be worshiped or idolized but they do *represent* such a great deal. I have saved, back home, a locket of my mother's hair but I do not bow before it as something holy. I keep it for the memories. I keep it to look at now and then and remember how beautiful she once was."

Brother Thaddeus perked up.

"And there is nothing wrong with hoarding such mementos, of course. In a different way, the bones of an apostle are a memento. We are human, and we need these links with the past. We need these reminders."

With a sweep of his arm, he indicated the other items in that room.

"The holy father decided to transfer as many as possible to safekeeping elsewhere. Some were so fragile that they could hardly be touched, let alone moved any distance at all. These were left where they were, and the guard detail doubled.

"This monastery was selected by Pope Adolfo personally to hold the remaining irreplaceable items, in fact, the greatest number. Of course, due to age some of the scrolls are so fragile that they cannot be unrolled without turning to dust. This site, while not impossibly far from the Vatican, is comparatively isolated. Secrecy is important."

"And Adolfo trusted *you*, is that not part of it?" Clarice complimented someone who exuded trustworthiness.

"It seems that way, though I feel exceedingly unequal to the task," he replied with a humility that seemed genuine.

"So what remains in Rome?" she asked, a logical question given the extent of what was stored in that one location.

"Relics."

"The bones of St. Peter?"

"How did you know that?" Brother Thaddeus asked.

"My father held some of them in his hands a few years ago."

"How blessed he must have been."

"If the circumstances had been different, he might have *felt* blessed, yes, but it was an awful time for him. He nearly died."

Brother Thaddeus was unaware of the details and respected Clarice's privacy by not inquiring further.

"I think we all should go outside now and see the situation in the valley," the monk suggested.

. . .*the situation in the valley*.

That was what forced them up the mountain and into the monastery in the first place.

Once the three had stepped out of the building itself, Clarice and Sarah stood for a moment and looked at it in awe once again. They had reached the ledge the night before but darkness had obscured much of the startling scope of that ancient building.

"How was it possible to erect this structure?" she asked the monk as she looked over the wall that reached from one side of the outer edge to the other, the drop just beyond it so extreme that she had to pull back or risk dizziness.

Brother Thaddeus chuckled.

"Certainly not up the path that you had to climb to get here."

Clarice blushed but was not miffed by that comment.

The so-called path he referred to had proved hardly an easy one to walk, even with nothing heavy to encumber them; simple, narrow manmade steps hewn into the rock, cracked by the passage of time and the not inconsiderable effects of erosion. Strong men could never navigate the path with any reasonable load of tools or anything else to carry that would be needed in the demanding process of building the monastery from scratch.

"The builders got everything they needed from the mountain itself," Brother Thaddeus told her.

"But tools and supplies," Sarah interjected, "what about those? With one man at a time climbing, it must have taken many, many months."

"There's a tunnel at the back," he said. "It is hidden by a tapestry hanging over it."

Clarice could imagine how scary that tunnel might be, with no natural light getting through it, only the light from torches providing enough for passage. She shivered at the thought, remembering what her father had told her about his nightmare in the catacombs under St. Peter's Basilica.

"But that is still a lot of climbing," she reminded him.

"They were men," Brother Thaddeus said, "and, as you know, men can do that which women cannot."

"It is men who cause wars," Sarah said, a bit provoked.

"Sometimes over the love of a woman!"

Despite his old-fashioned attitude, Clarice and Sarah liked Brother Thaddeus, a monk who could have played Friar Tuck in one of the traveling stage companies specializing in dramas about Robin Hood. They felt he was more honest than most of the men of whatever station they had met in their trips to Europe. And Brother Thaddeus was much more friendly than the other monks who seemed almost antagonistic toward anyone from the outside.

Sarah's gaze had drifted out over the four-foot-high stone wall, and as she looked down into the valley they had left a few hours before, she saw the rapid progression of what had driven them away in the first place.

Eden was being despoiled.

Over the years Clarice and Sarah had grown to love that particular valley and the cherished solitude that it offered. There they had known a lifestyle as serene as any that could be sustained in a modern, hectic, technological world, a world where an argument between individuals could become a war between countries.

*Our valley. . .*Clarice told herself. *Now it is a small version of what the world around us is becoming, with innocent people caught up in the madness. And it seems unlikely that it can ever be returned to what it once was.*

She found profoundly sad the fact that something precious was being spoiled, probably for all time.

Fights. . . .

Down in the valley people were fighting one another, spilling the blood of strangers. Often quaint, picturesque homes had been set ablaze, probably by accident since those who invaded the valley would have wanted places to stay, an alternative to being exposed to rains that were often heavy, and later, the blizzards.

"Eden is gone," Sarah said, genuinely regretful that a location she treasured could fall prey to ruin so quickly. "The serpent is here."

"Where the sin nature of each man and woman is present, there can *never* be paradise," the monk reminded her.

"But we have been coming here for years," Clarice told Brother Thaddeus. "It was so wonderful, so serene."

"And so there was no sin until now?" he asked. "No, it was never paradise here. Only the physical beauty created that illusion. You have no idea what was being practiced behind the walls of homes, however God-fearing your behavior happened to be."

Clarice and Sarah had hardly been sheltered by their parents, at least not like nuns in a convent, and this was because Cyril and Elizabeth Fothergill were convinced that any such approach meant that both daughters would be less capable of facing life when the inevitable hardships arose.

On the other hand, since the Fothergills led exemplary lives in matters moral, ethical, and spiritual, the two sisters had the best possible role models.

"We have heard of Cyril and Elizabeth Fothergill even here," Brother Thaddeus told them, intending no false flattery.

"You are just saying that to make us feel better," Clarice said.

"Rest assured I would not lie to make you feel better. I would not lie even to save your lives."

"But I would lie to save yours."

"And displease God at the same time."

"Yet save the lives of His dedicated servants," Clarice rejoined.

"There are other men like me, my dear, of that you can be certain. But none of us must ever endeavor to gain the virtuous by the sinful, for sin will never prove less than a stench in the nostrils of holiness."

Sarah let her attention turn again to the dreaded sights in the once-serene valley 2,000 feet below.

"Our chalet is gone!" she exclaimed, her eyes widening. "We should have stayed and fought along with the rest. We are nothing but cowards."

But Brother Thaddeus would not let her succumb to guilt.

"It is not cowardice to understand that there is no hope left," he told her, "that the horde breaking in upon you surely carried with it the strongest possibility of disease, disease that cannot be fought by what we know today.

"To have remained below would have been foolhardy, even suicidal, not brave. You both were wise. Just look at those people now, the ones you left behind, look at what they get for their so-called courage."

The three of them continued to survey the panorama before them, a valley that seemed virginal even if it were not, with smoke now rising up from one end to the other.

"The bodies!" Sarah said, nearly shouting, watching men and women drop and then lie still after being attacked.

"What you witness is to be expected," Brother Thaddeus replied sadly. "It will not be long before they find us."

"Find us?" Clarice asked. "This wall is made of rock, and it looks much like the mountain itself. The monastery is set back from view. How would they ever know?"

"The invaders might not. But you and your sister knew. So do others staying in the valley. Those who survive long enough will try to reach us and will be followed."

"What will you do?" Sarah asked. "Will you resist, fight?"

"We are peacemakers."

"Will you try to make peace then?"

"We shall."

The monk's expression showed that he had no real confidence of gaining the attention, let alone the salvation, of any intruders.

"You are going to die here, are you not, Brother Thaddeus?" Sarah asked, not cruelly but with sorrow.

"I expect to do that, yes."

"But my sister and I will run again."

"And again after that," the monk assured her. "You will keep on running because life is a gift from God."

"If it is a gift, and I agree with you that it is, then are you not throwing it away by remaining behind?" Sarah persisted.

Brother Thaddeus hesitated.

"How can you and the others hope to serve as peacemakers without turning your backs on this gift of life? Staying behind is an act of suicide. Where is the gift of life then? How can you continue to accept it without joining us when we leave?"

Clarice had not seen much of this side of her sister

before. And she found that she was enjoying its revelation.

"Should Christ have avoided the cross to linger for more years of spreading the Good News?" Brother Thaddeus countered.

"But Christ Jesus Himself *was* the Good News," Sarah replied. "With His death, burial, and Resurrection—"

Uncharacteristically, Brother Thaddeus interrupted.

"Please! Theology is hardly what I need to be taught," he retorted, but his basic humility caused him to instantly regret that flash of irritability. "Forgive me for such angry words. But I did surmise what you were about to say."

"Tell me what you think that was."

"That we should be dedicated to spreading the Good News as much as possible, and not closing ourselves off from the outside world."

His tone softened and he did not look directly at her.

"Yet that is not our mission here," he added. "Whatever my personal feelings, I have to obey the teachings of others."

"But what *is* your mission?" Sarah needed answers.

"To learn precious eternal truths from the ancient writings, to recopy as many of them as we can manage, so that none we possess will be lost during the ages to follow. Without the words of God dictated to His inspired scribes, how could we follow His wisdom? Is that not a mission worthy of God's safekeeping?"

Sarah walked around her sister and up to the monk.

"I want to whisper something into your ear," she said.

Puzzled but not perturbed, he bent over slightly.

"They will destroy everything when they make it to the ledge, you know," she told him without scorn. "How can God's wisdom be made available then? Yes, I know He can provide it any other way He wishes, but why make His work in this world more difficult, dear man? Which will happen if you remain here?"

Brother Thaddeus pulled back suddenly. He seemed in the throes of some kind of breakdown but his behavior did not go as far as that.

"You speak honestly, young woman," the monk said after he finally calmed himself down.

Now it was Sarah's turn to feel embarrassed.

"I'm sorry. . ." she said, hurrying back to stand beside her sister.

The screams from below were louder, and began echoing against the mountain surrounding the valley.

The monk looked over the edge and then faced the two sisters.

"It will be some while before they discover us," he said. "But it will happen. Somebody will reveal that we are here, and we will be seen as the perfect place to wait out the epidemic. Some will not want to harm us, but others, perhaps stricken, will be like madmen, taking out on the others and me what they see as God's unreasonable judgment on them.

"If we were to stay here, we *would* die by their hand, we should not doubt this for a moment, or perhaps from the virus itself, if not right away, then a week from now or a month, but it is going to happen.

"Nothing can stop what is transpiring. We have many memories of this spot but it is not one that can be saved for the future. What we had is gone forever. We must not be reluctant to leave if it is the Lord who is sending us elsewhere."

Both sisters were gratified that his thinking had changed.

Brother Thaddeus nodded toward the section of the monastery where the ancient scrolls were stored along with more recent copies.

"They will be wholly blinded, however distressing that is for the rest of us," he commented. "They will not see that knowledge, when it is knowledge of what God told the Old Testament prophets, and what Christ Himself later spoke of, *must* be preserved, whatever the level of sacrifice.

"Those people understand only that frightened family members and friends will require such rooms as we have here in which to stay, and that the very isolation of the monastery might give them a chance to avoid the epidemic.

"Such panic-stricken men and women will not be less than utterly, mindlessly consumed with the desperate need for survival at whatever cost to their decency, their morality, their *Christianity*.

"What my comrades and I have been blessed by learning since we came here so long ago, things of the mind and of the spirit, are unimportant to the men, women, and children below. Only survival will drive them, push them onward, with the corpses of the hapless in their wake."

Grieved by what Brother Thaddeus had said, Sarah felt nevertheless relieved that, after all, she had not made a fool of herself.

"So I was not wrong then?" she asked.

"Not at all," he acknowledged. "I was the one who was wrong, dear young woman, blind to a more sacred precept, in a sense, than the Great Commission itself. When there is no one around to spread its truths, when those truths become more and more obscure because there is less and less access to them, then—"

He stopped himself and bowed his head in prayer for a moment. When he looked up again at them, his eyes were wet.

"We may be entering a time when Satan will seek the greatest victories of his ever-cursed existence. The people have no hope of salvation except for the blessed truths of Scripture, *which must never be allowed to die out!*"

He had been speaking so forcefully that one of the other monks came out from the monastery and asked if anything were wrong.

"Sorry to interrupt," this one said sheepishly.

"When you go back in, tell the others we are leaving."

"For where, Brother Thaddeus?"

"The border of France, and just beyond it, to a home that was once a splendid fortress there, Brother Nathaniel."

"For a visit, all of us?"

Brother Thaddeus knew the wisdom of patience, and that his comrade sometimes required more than the usual share.

"To stay," he said kindly. "To stay for as long as we will find necessary, perhaps, if it so be, for the rest of our lives."

Brother Nathaniel, a skittish man who measured less than half the girth of Brother Thaddeus, and who wore a perpetually puzzled expression on his face, paused while trying to decide if he should say anything else. "Does it have anything to do with the commotion in the valley?" he asked finally.

"It has *everything* to do with that," Brother Thaddeus told him, a sense of urgency giving his words a sharper edge than he intended.

Again the slighter monk seemed lost for words and fidgeted conspicuously.

Brother Thaddeus had no time for indecision.

"What is it?" he asked. "We have little time to waste."

"The other brothers?"

A close relationship had existed between all twenty-two brothers for many years.

"Yes, what about them?"

Brother Thaddeus logically assumed that his fellow monks were also preparing to leave the monastery.

But where are they now? he thought.

It was then that he realized he had not seen any of the others for at least an hour, possibly longer.

"Are they spending a few last minutes in their quarters or the storage rooms?" he asked. "I should go to them, get them out here. We have so little time."

Brother Nathaniel shook his head.

"Unfortunately not," he replied.

"Then what *are* they doing?" Brother Thaddeus asked. "And where?"

The other monk was fighting to speak the words that he knew could not be deferred any longer.

"From what I can see," he said, "our friends are trying desperately to heed your many admonitions to be peace-makers."

Even Clarice and Sarah, not at all familiar with the

dictates the monks had been following since founding the monastery, or what the chain of command was, if any, caught the ominous thrust of that statement.

Brother Thaddeus grabbed the other monk by the shoulders.

"Please, I beg you, tell me that I am wrong to think what I *am* thinking," he exclaimed. "Please tell me that now."

Brother Nathaniel bowed his head, not able to answer, muted sobs escaping him.

Reluctantly, Clarice, closest to the wall that had been built around the outer side of the ledge, glanced over the edge.

Chaos reigned.

No matter how desperately she wanted to turn away, she stood transfixed as she witnessed the ghastly, bloody turmoil in a valley that once had seemed so virginal, the turmoil becoming greater by the minute, with innocent men, women, and children falling to the ground.

And those other monks, blind to the depravity of men. . .

Gentle men long ago pledging themselves to serving their Lord were being slaughtered even as they tried to bring peace!

Clarice had to turn away sharply.

"Brother Thaddeus," she said slowly. "Come here, will you?"

He studied her briefly, knowing that she would ask of him that which he already had refused to do.

"I cannot look," he replied. "I cannot allow myself to see what I surely will if I do what you have asked."

His pain was apparent.

"I know how you feel," she assured him. "But you must be a witness, you must know from what your own eyes tell you, not what someone else says. And the trail, Brother Thaddeus, the intruders have found it. I saw more than a dozen starting the climb already. There is no time to save anything. We must go now!"

He then walked over to the wall and looked in the direction that Clarice had been pointing.

"Blessed God!" he gasped in shock, nearly choking. "Blessed God Almighty, we are doomed if men can do that!"

He was mesmerized by the sight of the monks, those who had slipped away without his knowledge and gone down into the valley, as Clarice had said, and now were being consumed by the fires, the scene a reminder of the Roman treatment of Christians under the reign of Nero.

Brother Thaddeus folded his hands into fists and held them up toward the sky, shaking them angrily.

"My comrades. . .my dear, dear comrades! They all devoted their lives to Thee, O Heavenly Father!" he screamed pitiably. "Why take them all so cruelly? I know they go to be with Thee, and must no longer toil in this blighted world. But how could You allow Your servants to suffer so abominably?"

Seconds later, Brother Thaddeus nearly doubled over from the anguish that he was feeling, tears pouring down his cheeks.

Clarice walked over to the monk and he leaned his large form against her smaller, thinner one.

"May God forgive me for my rage," Brother Thaddeus mumbled. "May He in His mercy forgive me. I feel so ashamed!"

With great hesitation, Brother Nathaniel approached the wall and slowly glanced over its edge as well.

Only a few seconds passed before he turned away and became sick to his stomach in front of the others.

Still trembling, Brother Thaddeus sat down next to him. "There is an answer, there has to be an answer. Anger will not save us. All we have left is our faith."

Minutes later. . .

Clarice had been looking down into the valley, at the both pitiable and horrifying sight of humanity near madness.

"They are at least halfway up," she observed. "I looked

before coming inside."

Brother Thaddeus seemed to be in another world.

"Do you know what we have endured here in service to God?" the monk asked calmly. "We raise our own crops season after season. We sometimes kill game that happens by, mountain goats and rabbits and a few others."

He was proud of this ability to sustain themselves as well as they had been doing since the monastery was built.

"We drink as much cool water as we want from a mountain stream," he continued. "We have wine in the cellar that the Vatican sends in periodically, along with some wonderful cheeses from Switzerland and Germany. And—" he paused, as if in the middle of a Shakespearean soliloquy.

"We have endured much pain, through injuries and sickness and, sometimes, hunger and thirst as when the crops have failed, however careful we are with them, or when the game do not appear, when the stream temporarily was choked off and when the wine was delayed."

But these were just some of the problems that such a group of men faced, during the beginning years.

"And there has been the loneliness, not a small matter. This has decreased decade by decade because of the bonding that has occurred between us. Though we are seldom alone as such, what with so many comrades here, and so much activity to keep us alive, we still have known loneliness, together with everything else. It is a constant threat, and more debilitating than the worst nature can throw against us.

"As a result, we all have been strengthened, physically as well as spiritually. Tough? Yes, we are. My comrades and I have felt for most of our adult life that there is nothing in Scripture that says the meek are *not* to be strong of will and body and spirit, that they should be weak by their very nature, and vacillating, hardly deserving respect or any valid conviction that they ever *could* inherit the earth. To prevail, the meek *must* have a strength that perhaps other men do not, strength to surmount the difficulties that are part of life on this sin-cursed world. We have never doubted this and we never shall."

Abruptly, Brother Thaddeus brought his hand to his mouth.

"Every last one must be dead now!" he gasped.

His eyes had widened as he realized how he had been talking about the other monks, as though little had changed.

"What a foolish soul I am!" he exclaimed. "I have been going on as though none of what once existed here has changed or will change. Yet every bit of it has been thrown away. We will never meet again in *this* world. We—"

After shaking his head several times as though to rid himself of a sudden and brutal wave of mourning and a depression closing in such as he had never known before then, Brother Thaddeus remarked, "May Almighty God, in His mercy and grace, give all of us the strength to get through what lies ahead."

The four of them then hurried down a long bare hallway to another location at the northwestern corner of the monastery, stopping in front of the wall where the only entrance to the tunnel they sought was hidden.

It was still difficult for the monks to leave.

They both had spent many years in that one location. The items they were supposed to study as well as guard would be left behind to an uncertain fate. In light of that, their ambivalence was understandable.

"History is no longer important, it seems," Brother Nathaniel lamented. "But history is all we have."

"An appreciation for history never is indispensable during such times as these," the other monk mused. "When people are fighting for their survival, only the harsh demands of the present matter. You can hardly blame them for choosing survival over what are to them just dusty old scrolls."

Brother Nathaniel was disgusted, not realizing that his fellow monk was simply playing devil's advocate.

"You could hardly blame them if they were mere brute beasts, with no concept of the past or the future," he said. "But they are human beings created in the image of God!"

Sarah felt outclassed in such company, and realistically speaking, there was a measure of truth in this, but still she asked, "May I say something?"

"Of course," Brother Thaddeus told her.

"We aren't able to stay, I know that," she began. "While I really can imagine how you both feel, don't you think that if God does want anything preserved, He will see to it that this happens somehow?"

She was being simplistic, even Clarice was aware of that.

"But He also expects us to be loyal guardians," Brother Nathaniel replied, with a slight edge of condescension in his tone. "We are hardly to be helpless before the enemy, yet here we are, running away."

He was frustrated at being forced into the course of action he had decided to take.

Unwisely Sarah persisted.

"Yet what is most important?" she asked. "Manuscripts centuries old or human life? You chastise people who choose their loved ones and themselves above your archives. Are they 'mere brute beasts,' as you have said, or instead, are they obeying instincts for preservation, for defense of their families that God instilled in them in the first place?"

The monk shrugged his shoulders and closed his eyes, signaling the end of his participation in any such discussion, while Brother Thaddeus smiled helplessly, his very manner asking tolerance for his friend's attitude.

As for Clarice, she remained out of the little debate but rather proud of her sister showing a side of her personality that ironically had come out only in the company of strangers.

Clarice had been sitting on the floor, using their laptop computer.

"*No!*" she exclaimed.

The others were startled.

"What is wrong, young woman?" Brother Thaddeus asked.

"Prime Minister Edling ordered the sinking of a boat

that was approaching Portsmouth," Clarice told them.

"There must be some mistake," Brother Nathaniel said.

"There was the very real chance that some of the people were virus-infected."

"How could he *know* that?" Brother Thaddeus spoke again. "Even so, how—?"

He could not continue speaking. Nor, in fact, could his fellow monk or Sarah, both of whom were dealing with images of men, women, and children dying in the English Channel just as they were so close to what they hoped was a haven of safety.

CHAPTER 2

Clarice and Sarah Fothergill and the monks began the long and tedious journey through the very center of the mountain and were now more than halfway across into France without mishap or complication. This feat seemed miraculous in itself since the winding tunnel that the four were navigating was devoid of any natural light except for what was shed by their torches. Together they faced its atmosphere of eeriness, which was aided by nearly continual and always disturbing sounds from whatever animal or insect existed within its confines, compounded by odors that bespoke decay and rot.

Yet two out-of-condition monks traveling with two inexperienced young women were determined to make it to the end in good spirits.

Until one of the sisters had a sudden and terrifying bout with claustrophobia, the first she had ever experienced. . . .

Clarice had stopped walking and was sitting on the cold, moist earth "floor," her head buried in her hands.

Shivering.

At first Sarah thought this might have been happening because of the cold temperature of that musty tunnel.

"No!" Clarice told her. "I. . .I have to get out of here. I have to leave this horrid place. Please believe me!"

Brother Thaddeus approached her.

"What is wrong here?" he asked.

"My sister. . ." Sarah started to tell the monk. "She seems not like herself at all. She has not acted this way before now."

Clarice looked up at them.

"It is like death down here," she said, her tone pleading. "Things have *died* in this tunnel—we have kicked against their bones, we have smelled the odors—probably as long ago as hundreds or thousands of years."

They had seen an array of bones, some part of fairly intact skeletons, others not much more than dust.

"We are walking through what amounts to an unmarked graveyard," Clarice said. "It is all around us. . .the smell. . . the—"

Some three years earlier she had been deeply affected by her father's harrowing account of his experiences in the catacombs of St. Peter's Basilica.

I was nineteen years old, she thought, *too young to understand fully but too old to forget his anguish.*

Cyril Fothergill had withheld few details since he believed that avoiding the truth only guaranteed that the opportunity for it could be resurrected later under circumstances that might not be as easily controlled.

"He almost died down there," she went on. "And we are in a place similar to where he was. What if—?"

Their normal roles reversed, Sarah sat with Clarice and tried to talk her out of whatever was assaulting her mind.

"But we do not face a madman," she said softly.

They had tried not to think of Baldasarre Gervasio since their father had returned from that ordeal years before.

"And he is not sending hundreds of rats against us," she continued. "We have two new friends with us. We are not as helpless as Father became."

"I know," Clarice agreed. "There is a difference this time. You do not have to remind me of that. But I cannot help myself, Sarah. I think I have always feared places like this. We could die down here and never be found. And then what would happen to our parents? It would destroy them, losing us like that."

It was Brother Nathaniel's turn to speak.

"We know about this man you mention," he said. "The holy father is blinded to the evil nature that some of us seem able to recognize. But Brother Thaddeus and I will not give up until he is stopped."

The monk looked at Clarice with such apparent compassion that his very countenance seemed to calm her down.

"Your father was alone, I gather," he said, showing another part of himself that the two sisters had not seen previously.

"Completely alone."

In one sense, Cyril Fothergill had known that he was not alone, that a host of angels did surround him, and the Holy Spirit indwelt him. But that was the spiritual side of his nature. The other, very much physical, the side of him that could see the darkness, that could hear the sound of little claws on rock, that could smell centuries of death and decay, that could sense the presence of creatures ready to submerge him beneath a suffocating pile of their stinking bodies, this side had seemed as utterly alone as any human being could be.

"But *you* are not alone, my dear, not by any means," Brother Nathaniel observed. "You have my brother and me with you. And you have your sister. And this is a tunnel that will lead us to safety. I know it well. We have had to memorize every foot. We have never seen rats or spiders or snakes or any other creatures that could harm us."

She noticed that he had pressed his hands together as though in prayer.

"Think of it not as a place of fear," he remarked, "think of it instead as a blessed gift from Almighty God."

In a moment Clarice somehow had been able to will herself to be far calmer, but she was still ashamed of the way she had displayed her weakness in front of others whose respect she could not afford to lose.

"You must think me weak," she said, her voice hardly louder than a whisper, "you must find me a disgrace."

Brother Nathaniel objected, denying any such thoughts.

"Do not be ashamed of having felt fear after you have conquered it," the monk told her. "If we had no enemies, we would never have to go to war. We are here because our enemies are after us, the ones we can see, the other now invisible. Anyone who claims no fear is either a liar or a fool. And you are neither."

Brother Nathaniel had had to deal with fear a number of times during his years at the monastery, the fear of pleasing God. Though he had devoted all of his adult life trying to satisfy what he felt were God's unchangeable conditions, the monk could not feel at peace, could not get the sense that the Creator was anything but annoyed with him.

I pray to You at night, he would say to himself, *but I get no comfort when I do, no communication that tells me, "Dear child of the King, I accept your deeds and you may rest with the peace that passes all understanding."*

Here I am, Heavenly Father, denying myself that which others would call the simplest of human pleasures in the hope of approaching a state of righteousness, but You seem not to notice what I am doing or care. You seem instead to ignore what must seem like pitiable utterances.

While some of the other monks felt as Brother Nathaniel, most had learned the value of simple acceptance, of believing that God was happy with their efforts, without any need for Him to say so directly.

"I am not so sure that I *have* conquered it," she told him. "I think I must take this quite slowly, step by step."

"Conquered?" Brother Nathaniel repeated, straining with the effort of trying to camouflage how greatly his mind had drifted back to those circumstances he himself had been facing since entering the monastery ten years before. "You are not supposed to be without human emotion when you are a Christian. And fear is one of those. Any loss of emotion makes us less than human in the way God intended. And is that not life itself? One step, then another, and finally, Lord willing, the victory we have sought."

They did not feel victorious at that point. They were cold, they were tired, and the only light, from their torches, was dwindling. None wanted to be in the total darkness of that tunnel, no matter how safe it had been done until then.

But Brother Nathaniel was doing his best, for the others as well as himself, and at the same time, the Lord he served.

Life had taken an abrupt and tragic turn for Clarice and Sarah, accustomed as they were to having whatever happened in their private world carefully controlled. Now none of that mattered, and they both could not resist wondering if they would ever again be able to sleep without being afraid.

Three-quarters of the way through the tunnel. . .

Clarice, Sarah, and the two monks came upon what appeared to be the ravaged remains of three small children.

"How could they be here without anyone in the monastery knowing what was going on?" Clarice speculated.

Brother Thaddeus cleared his throat.

"Remember, this tunnel was conceived of as an escape route. There was no justification for anyone to venture into the tunnel to this distance."

He shrugged his shoulders.

"The only reason to enter other than escape could be curiosity, and I can picture no one being so curious that they would stay here for long."

Clarice persisted, driven by the poignancy of what she saw.

"But these were innocent children, very small, very young, very helpless," she said. "And look at what happened to them. Look at it! The bones in each case seem to have been torn apart, scattered in several directions. . .like they were used in some ritual."

Sarah had wandered ahead a few yards.

"Come here," they heard her call.

The monks and Clarice sidestepped the children's remains and hurried to where Sarah was standing.

A fire. Or rather what had been a fire.

"Sacrifice. . ." Brother Nathaniel stated simply.

"Druids?" Clarice asked.

"Not likely. The Druids prefer newborn flesh. Besides, they have never been the only ones to take children for such purposes."

"Not the only—" Sarah repeated, blanching at this new

information, information that she found difficult to accept.

"But why?" she asked, incredulous. "Why would they take young children and burn them to death over a fire?"

"Their cries, I think," Brother Nathaniel replied.

"They *enjoy* hearing the cries of dying children?"

Sarah turned away, the absolute perversity of that truth hitting her as though a large rock were slamming into her jaw.

Brother Nathaniel's reply did not help.

"I believe so," he said, "however macabre that sounds."

Sarah had bent down and picked up something from the pile of ashes. . .a gold crucifix.

"One of the little ones must have been Christian," she said, closing her fingers around it as she pressed her hand against her chest.

"That child is now beyond pain," Brother Thaddeus said. "Rejoice in that, my friends, rejoice in that, if nothing else."

And so the four of them plodded the rest of the way through that ancient and cramped tunnel, eventually emerging from it at the southwestern border of France.

CHAPTER 3

The demonic scheme could not be called less than ingenious.

While the rats were being kept beneath St. Peter's, they were exceptionally robust, well fed, and propagating at a dynamic rate, with Baldasarre Gervasio making sure of the quality of their care. Any helper, priest or otherwise, who did not do as the rat man directed could count on being severely disciplined.

Just as the now thousands of rats were being readied for shipment throughout Europe, additional hundreds were being brought in from China by clandestine means and intermingled with the ostensibly healthy rodents.

The dangerous ones.

The newcomers had been known to be rather sickly and were suspected of carrying the epidemic, according to reports from places in Asia where the hantavirus seemed a perpetual hazard. Many had died during the long trip but many did manage to survive, and give birth to another generation that was capable of carrying the disease but immune to it, which delighted the men behind the plot because it meant that they would need fewer rats.

Within a day scores upon scores of crates containing the healthy as well as the infected rats were sent to key population centers in every country on the continent, some by truck and some by boat.

But there was more to it than that.

A false story was cleverly circulated by word of mouth, namely that the virus came in accidentally through seaports in the south of Italy and France where, it was said, reasonable sanitary conditions did not exist, and if there were any hope of making safe the rest of the continent as well as the British Isles, all ports had to be sealed off.

Attempted extermination of the creatures began at every

harbor, major or otherwise, along the Mediterranean, the Atlantic Ocean, and the English Channel. This kind of multinational action involved uncustomary coordination by the various governments, a coordination that was surprisingly easy to arrange given the stakes for each of the countries involved, and there were glowing pronouncements of the expected success of their efforts.

Nothing.

Since that had been believed, these efforts produced no lessening impact whatever where the epidemic was concerned.

All of this occurred three years after the initial scare, three years for people to come to believe that it was a hoax, nothing more, three years to become complacent. . . .

The village rested on an open expanse of fertile land not much more than a mile from where that section of the French Alps ended. It seemed to be everything that Clarice, Sarah, and the two monks could have wanted after their ordeal: quiet and isolated, indeed, a fine place in which they could rest and regain their strength for the rest of the journey. From a distance, it appeared as idyllic as the one the sisters used to cherish, drawing them to it year after year.

Clarice stood and gazed at the inviting little homes and the larger buildings where various businesses were conducted, and so did her sister and the two monks, none of them with less relief that they had found such a place.

So beautiful, Clarice thought with a wistfulness born of longing to be back home and safe. *But what will we find when we enter it?*

But there was more to the scene than the village alone.

A vineyard, a vast vineyard.

The rolling expanse of vines stretched out in every direction, with the village surrounded by these on all sides, three paths leading through the vineyard to the houses and stores.

"This area is not known for wine, strangely enough," Brother Thaddeus remarked. "It is the grapes themselves that are sought."

Clarice was surprised by that.

"But I thought wine was more profitable," she said.

"Yes, but grapes in their natural form are an important part of the local diet, and here in this region in particular, the grapes themselves are most highly prized because they have an especially vibrant taste."

Clarice was hungry and the thought of eating some fresh fruit outside under a clear sky was enormously appealing.

"In England, most people can't afford to eat grapes as they are so expensive to import," she said.

Brother Thaddeus approached one of the tallest vines and, without hesitation, started picking some grapes from it.

"They belong to somebody!" Sarah protested, alarmed that he was doing something illegal. "Should you be going after them like that?"

He chuckled knowingly.

"The ones that are intended for private use, including sale, are on the other side of the village," the monk told her. "These are for anyone who wants them."

His expression showed how charming he thought this was, as he added, "It is the villagers' way of welcoming visitors."

Knowing that, the two sisters eagerly joined with both monks in consuming bunches of the red-skinned grapes.

A short while later, sitting on the ground, they all were feeling better, content even to the point of dozing off for a brief period.

Smoke. . . .

Faintly at first, so faint that it could be overlooked, and sleep continued. But then stronger.

A cloud of dense smoke.

Carried by the gentlest of breezes through the vineyard, the odor awakened them, though for Clarice and Sarah there was more of a shock than for Brothers Thaddeus and Nathaniel.

All four jumped to their feet.

"It smells so much like what we found at that site where the Druids were having their sacrifices," Clarice observed uneasily, not able to bury completely what had happened that night. "The same awful burning of—"

Brother Thaddeus had become nervous.

"This is serious," he said, overhearing what she had said. "This is very serious."

"What do you mean?" Clarice asked.

"You spoke of Druids. . ." Brother Thaddeus repeated. "What experience have you had with their kind?"

She gave him a brief recap of what had happened at Woodhenge.

"I am not surprised," the monk replied. "They are little more than miserably enslaved demonic puppets who have skillfully deluded many people. They seem to me far, far worse than the Muslims ever will be."

Clarice found that difficult to accept.

"Why do you say that?" she asked. "Their numbers seem insignificant. How can you even compare the two?"

"*Every* Druid is fanatically devoted to the demise of Christianity," Brother Thaddeus said with some authority.

"Is that out of revenge for eventually being overwhelmed by the spread of Christianity?" Sarah asked.

"I think it is much deeper than that," the monk continued. "They were hostile even at the beginning, during the earthly ministry of Christ. I suspect that one or more of them was a member of Pilate's government, under the guise of Roman counselors.

"While the proconsul's wife desperately wanted to free Jesus, her husband was getting the strongest contrary advice from quite another quarter, perhaps a mysterious Druid, largely ignored in the historical records, who had been close to the emperor and was sent to the Holy Land to make sure that Pilate would not give in to his better instincts."

"Is it possible that the Druids believed Christ's message more than the people of Israel?" Clarice asked. "But they rebelled against it, and tried to secure His death?"

The monk nodded solemnly.

"They could see in Jesus Christ the seeds that, if planted, would result in the destruction of their sect," he replied. "These people had a certain satanic wisdom, though they could not peer into the future. They could, however, feel the power that came from Him, the divinity that was so unmistakable to any whose eyes were not blinded."

Brother Thaddeus had studied the Druids and their beliefs as well as their rites for many years and he knew more about them than Pope Adolfo.

"Druids have invariably shown themselves to be most interested in the summoning of occultic spirits and the practice of voodoolike rites. In fact, they offer in a straightforward, undiluted manner what the Muslims only hint at. Frankly, it strains credulity for me to believe that many Muslims are involved in this epidemic, certainly not their leaders. You see, before I became a monk, and even after that, I did enjoy the company of some fine Muslim friends."

A haughty streak in Clarice surfaced.

"I doubt that my family and I ever had anything to do with any Muslim," she said. "I am unable to remember meeting even one."

Brother Thaddeus deemed it best to ignore that comment.

"While I could never begin to agree in any way with any important aspect of their theology, of course, I found them as people to be law-abiding, rather pleasant men and women who seemed very much at peace with themselves and the world around them.

"Oh, I could certainly argue most strongly about why these individuals, and others like them, felt this way, particularly the part that delusion played in their lives, but there was no denying that they did possess something that could be called peace even if it did not stem from a scriptural foundation. Accordingly, I would go so far as to say that they would have been appalled if they had learned about anything as monstrous or demonic as a master plan designed to wipe out Christian Europe."

But no one could stop it now.

Baldasarre Gervasio's rats had been released from the bowels of the Vatican.

They were not smart when compared to such other creatures as dogs, cats, and horses, but that was perhaps one of their greatest weapons. Vicious when cornered, the rats could be loyal when treated well, a loyalty that, in its blindness, made them do anything they were trained to do, no matter what the cost to themselves.

And they seemed to like the rat man—and hate anyone who got in his way. His wrath became theirs. He could be trusted to feed them well, to stand among them unafraid, even as they swarmed over him, almost to the point of submerging him beneath their bodies.

Instead of being repulsed, instead of trying to run afraid from their midst, he relished their attention, for they did not care about his appearance or understand any purpose of his except as it translated into food for them, food that they did not have to spend hours hunting down.

And so they stayed with him, breeding more and more of their kind, a thousand becoming two thousand becoming four thousand becoming eight thousand.

On and on the population grew until there was scarcely enough space to contain them.

A few within the Vatican knew about the rats. But they were the rat man's puppets, either in league with him out of admiration, if that could be imagined, or from fear of what he was capable of inflicting upon them if he detected that they were restless.

Someday Pope Adolfo would find out.

But until that happened, the rat man held sway over a domain and an army that would spread destruction across the continent and beyond.

CHAPTER 4

As they traversed country roads, away from any major population centers and often through thick forests, they saw no one else, alive, that is, only overturned automobiles, twisted bicycles, and the remains of bodies that had been dead for a long time.

Finally, though, they saw a village ahead, one that was difficult to avoid. . . .

A fire, undoubtedly the source of the smoke that had disturbed their sleep. Far worse than the one set by Druids years before, coming from an apparently deep pit that had been dug over a period of days in the village square.

"Anything they could gather up that burns is surely resting at the bottom," Brother Thaddeus wisely observed from where he was crouched. "Every able-bodied man, woman, and child must have joined together digging that pit, and taking away the dirt. Then when it was completed, they surely had to use hay, wood, clothes, anything.

"And they will need all of this and whatever else they can locate to keep it as hot as possible for as long as they can. Nothing must be left but ashes. Any bones are to be smashed to dust by rocks thrown over the edge."

"And that will be enough to stop the virus?" Clarice asked, knowing few of the details about the disease itself.

Unsure of the answer, the monk shrugged his shoulders.

"No one knows for certain," Brother Thaddeus said. "Fire has cleansed disease from the earth at other times, of course. But the hantavirus seems so very different from the rest. It spreads far more rapidly. And it consumes the sufferer so quickly that they must feel as though they have been overrun by a horde of demons."

Sunlight was fading as dusk approached. Human figures entered the square to throw more items into the pit and then raced away again.

At first only the sound of the flames could be heard, until—

Cries. . . .

Faint at first, then stronger. People being *dragged* into the square.

Clarice, Sarah, and the two monks were crouched on the ground, watching this sight from the vantage point of a small hill that overlooked the village.

"They are still alive!" Clarice exclaimed.

"But suffering from the hantavirus!" Brother Thaddeus pointed out. "Healthy people are not inclined to take any chances. As horrible as that sounds, the whole mob has become convinced it is the only way they can survive. There is a ghastly logic to what they say, however cruel or barbaric."

"But is it like this everywhere?" Sarah asked. "In so short a time have people given up their humanity?"

"I pray not. I pray that some semblance of Christian heritage can be salvaged throughout the continent. Otherwise, there will be little difference between living here and living in a jungle."

"And Britain. . ." she muttered. "Britain as well?"

"Indeed, Britain as well."

They returned their attention to the scene ahead of them, perhaps out of a fascination that was not healthy but they were unable to turn away.

Over the edge. . . .

In front of them, body after body was being tossed into the flames, whether dead or alive, it did not seem to matter to those assigned the task of disposal.

But not all the living stayed among the consuming flames, quickly dying. Some, their bodies on fire, tried pulling themselves up the side of the pit. Those who made it to the top were pushed back in by the villagers stationed there.

"*Gehenna. . .*" Brother Nathaniel muttered.

Both Clarice and Sarah felt cold, as much from what

the monk had said as from a sudden fall breeze.

One man. . . .

He had escaped the flames altogether and managed to climb out of the pit, standing quietly for a moment as he tried to steady himself.

His body was bloated and bruised. And the sores! The telltale, grotesque sores. On his chest and down his back.

Sarah had to close her eyes, unable, even from a distance, to look any longer.

Two villagers had started approaching the man for the purpose of dragging him back to the pit, with no intention of allowing him to pull himself up from the flames this time.

"He laughs!" Sarah, stunned, exclaimed. "How can he be laughing? Has this one been driven quite mad?"

The two monks murmured agreement.

The man did nothing but stand there, hands defiantly on his hips, and simply laugh at the village men who were coming for him, a coarse laugh it was, desperate arrogance apparent, and yet there was no raising of his mottled fists in defense.

The villagers stopped several feet in front of him, trying to see if he had found some weapon and was concealing it. But he had nothing in his grasp that seemed able to do injury, no rock or knife, or any clothes with pockets.

"You are not being invited to a party," one of the villagers growled scornfully at him. "Stop that laughing! You mock your fate. Have you no shame before all of us here?"

"No shame?" he repeated. "You are the ones suffering from a lack of shame. You give me no chance to live. Is that not the most shameful act of all, denying me the right to recover from this horrible malady?"

"The epidemic claims all who catch it!" one of the villagers yelled back at him. "We are trying to protect those as yet uninfected. Can you not understand why we must be careful, why we cannot allow compassion to dissuade us?"

He continued his utterly bizarre behavior, laughing

insanely, while shouting at them until they stepped forward, hands curled into fists, two of them holding clubs, the man on the left carrying a particularly brutal-looking ax that he seemed ready to use, unless he was bluffing, or ignorant of the fact that axing anyone to death meant scattering the victim's blood, which guaranteed the spread of the virus. They all were being governed by panic, panic that smothered their common sense.

Dear God, Brother Thaddeus prayed. *Dear God, I think he is going to—*

And then he did what the monk suspected.

He responded in a manner that on other occasions would have been considered a terrible insult, but not deadly. However, the epidemic had made it as potentially fatal as shooting them with arrows or stabbing them in the heart.

He spat at both villagers, hitting each man in the face.

"That was what I thought he would do, to strike back for what they were doing to him," Brother Thaddeus whispered. "I can understand his rage, and the idea of disposing of a living human being in that order is barbaric though there is some sense to it, however awful. But he is hardly prepared to listen, and give in."

"But surely those other men will be infected," Sarah observed.

"That was his purpose, my dear," Brother Thaddeus told her.

She fell into silence.

"In a few days both of them will be dead," the monk said solemnly.

The man seemed to be savoring his temporary survival, adrenaline giving him strength that the virus had robbed from him, for he approached those hapless other individuals in the square, men and women standing around either out of concern for dead or dying relatives or friends, or from perverse curiosity.

He spat at some, grabbed one of the prettier middle-aged women and kissed her, and tried, it seemed, to contaminate as many others as he could before someone drove a knife through his chest. Ironically, in that moment of dying, his blood spurting out, he was able to infect several more, including the one who slayed him, until finally his body was dumped once again into the vile pit.

CHAPTER 5

Nighttime came after what seemed like a very long day, a day in which the travelers questioned what could possibly be ahead of them.

. . .to contaminate as many others as he could before someone drove a knife through his chest.

The four of them were shaken by what they had witnessed.

"I remember the notion that we all would evolve into better beings," Brother Nathaniel mused as they walked. "Religion wasn't needed because evolution would carry everyone to a higher moral, ethical plain."

He grunted in contemptuous dismissal, and lapsed into silence.

None of them talked further until they settled down for the night, in a clearing surrounded by forest growth, having seen it from the road and judged it to be promising, especially the little stream running through it.

The monks had salvaged some food from the monastery stores, as well as some blankets, and so they would not starve for a few days, or freeze.

About midnight. . . .

Sounds.

They all heard rustling sounds in the undergrowth, loud enough to break through the half-sleep that the four had managed to slip into after their systems wound down from everything that had happened earlier.

"Animals!" Clarice exclaimed.

They carried no weapons.

An attack from unknown predators could occur and they would have nothing with which to defend themselves.

The sounds did not come from night creatures.

Human faces appeared between the trees, young, pale

faces, bloodshot eyes staring at them.

Brother Thaddeus stood and called out to them, "Children, children, we will not harm you! Please—!"

Laughter. Cold, sad, cruel.

And a voice.

"We've heard that before!" it exclaimed. "You're a priest, aren't you?"

"Yes, I—" the rotund monk started to reply.

"I was raped by a priest a few years ago," the voice continued, "then he passed me along to some other men like him. Until the little rat man put a stop to it, and befriended us!"

. . .*the little rat man.*

Clarice and Sarah both gasped as they heard those words and glanced at Brother Nathaniel who put a finger to his lips, urging them to be quiet.

"What are you doing here?" Brother Thaddeus asked.

"Looking. . ." another voice said.

The voice sounded like a computer simulation, not anything that was actually human.

"For what?"

"Fun."

"Fun? In the world like it is?"

"What more is there?"

To the monk, that remark had the same effect as the sound of chalk slowly being scraped across a blackboard.

"Your survival," Brother Thaddeus said. "We have to get through this nightmare, all of us."

"My kind may *never* survive, fat man!"

"How can you say that?"

"When people find out the truth," the voice said, a slight trembling in it now.

"What truth?"

There was laughter again.

"We have only one hope," it said.

"Yes, there is only one source of hope," Brother Nathaniel interjected, thinking of salvation through Jesus Christ.

"Not the One you mean."

"How do you know what I am thinking of?"

"You're a priest. I used to believe what adults shoved down my throat."

"Then what? What do you think is your only hope?"

"Killing."

The others signaled their agreement as they shouted, "Yeah! That's right."

"You think murder is the answer?"

"If we get rid of all our enemies, we will be the only ones left."

"Are you going to kill us now?"

"Yes!"

The undergrowth was rustling with activity. Faint figures took shape as they stepped into the clearing.

Young people, as Brothers Thaddeus and Nathaniel and the two sisters already knew, that much was no longer a shock to the four adults.

Except the way these teenagers looked.

Scrawny, covered with scars, one with his arm hanging lifelessly at his side, another with a patch over one eye.

Most wore clothes that were dirty and torn and some were without shirts, revealing nearly emaciated chests.

All were boys.

And every last one of the half dozen were armed with long-bladed knives, pistols, or machetes.

"What has happened to you?" Brother Thaddeus asked, genuinely disturbed.

The tallest boy, obviously the leader, stepped forward, smirking.

"I think this God of yours must have been looking the other way."

Sarah spoke up this time.

"If the rat man were taking care of you, what went wrong?" she asked. "You all are in miserable shape. And you must be very hungry."

"We discovered what was really in his head," the leader replied.

"Tell us. . ." Brother Thaddeus urged, having learned that getting distraught people to talk was the easiest way to deter them from acts of anger.

It did not work this time.

"I know what you're doing," the leader retorted. "We're not so dumb, you know. Fighting to survive against our parents, then the rat race, and now the virus has toughened us up, made us smarter."

"I do not doubt that," Brother Thaddeus continued, "but—"

"But nothin'!" the leader told him.

Sarah walked up and stood in front of him.

"How old are you?" she asked, sympathetic to an extent that her sincerity could not be questioned.

"Sixteen."

"I'm only four years older. Don't you think I have some feeling for what you've been telling us?"

The leader shook his head disdainfully.

"You're lucky."

"I don't believe in luck."

"What then? God's will or something?"

"God's will, yes."

"What about His will when we were suffering so much?"

"There are no answers because the questions have to be asked in faith."

"Double-talk."

"My mother may be dying. I don't know why. I just love God more than I have *ever* doubted Him. Have I *ever* doubted? Of course!"

The leader looked at her then spat in her face.

"That's what I think of your faith."

Sarah did not flinch.

"My name is Sarah Fothergill," she told him, extending her hand, "and I forgive you for that."

"My name is Dwayne Pederson, and I forgive you *nothing*!" he replied.

One of the other boys leaned over and whispered something to him. His eyes widened, and he stepped back.

"Your name is Sarah *Fothergill*?"

"Yes. . .it is," Sarah replied.

"Your father is Cyril Fothergill?"

"Yes. . .yes, he is."

In an instant, every teenager had either sheathed his knife or holstered his pistol.

The monks glanced at one another, surprise written on their faces.

"I can't believe this," Dwayne Pederson said, seeming more like the awestruck fan of a rock-and-roll star.

"What's going on?" Clarice finally asked. "Do you know our father?"

"The rat man hated Cyril Fothergill. He *feared* him, too."

"Why?"

"He never said, but we overheard conversations. When we ran away from him, he was planning to send assassins into England, to hunt down your father."

The two sisters were stunned.

"I think I know why," Sarah said. "Let's sit down and talk about it."

All of the teenaged boys agreed without protest.

Throwing up their hands in amazement, Brothers Thaddeus and Nathaniel joined them.

"Go ahead," Pederson told Sarah.

"Our father has the ability to lead people," she said.

"So does the rat man."

"Not really. For him, it's all intimidation. That's not leadership. With our father, it grows out of respect and trust."

The teenagers were nodding.

"He tricked us," Pederson said. "He made us believe that he was interested in making life better for everybody."

"Deception is a ready tool of the wicked," Brother Thaddeus said.

"You ain't seen nothin' wicked until you've been with

the rat race!" exclaimed one of the other boys.

"You said a little while back that you discovered what he was really up to," Sarah reminded him.

"Yes, we did. He wanted revenge. He convinced us that we could have it, too. What he didn't tell anybody was that he was willing to sacrifice everyone around him so long as he got what *he* wanted!"

"Doesn't he realize that if he's the only one left, revenge is going to come back and destroy him as well?"

"He had that covered."

"What do you mean?"

"There's a group that he was preparing."

"What sort of group?"

"The smartest ones, the ones who could run computers," Pederson recalled, shivering. "Everybody else was expendable."

Oddly enough, Sarah felt a sudden chill settle over her body as well.

"What in the world did he want them for?" she asked.

"We never knew."

"No clues."

"We were the ones who did most of the grunt work. Sending out the rats was a duty most of us had."

His expression was dark, haunted.

"We would pretend that they were just pets, but when no one was looking, we'd release all of them."

"Where?"

"Everywhere throughout Italy, you name it: Sicily, Florence, Milan, Rome, and over the northern border into the rest of Europe."

"But if they were infected, what about the risk?"

"Some of the kids died, yeah, but we knew that going in."

"Who was pulling Gervasio's strings? I can't believe that he alone devised everything. My father was told that Muslims were behind it all, and that the rat man was just capitalizing on what they already had set in motion. Is that what you think?"

"We've never had reason to question it."

Pederson signaled for the others to stand as he was now doing. "We gotta go now."

"But why?" Sarah asked. "Why can't we stay together?"

"Whatever is left of the authorities is on to us," he told her.

Brother Thaddeus stepped forward.

"We could intercede for you," he pleaded. "Pope Adolfo could—"

"No, it would never happen. We've done a lot of crime, even after leaving the rat man. We have been surviving any way we could."

"But there is forgiveness," the monk stressed, desperately trying to head off what seemed an inevitable disaster.

"God may forgive me, but not the people whose homes we have robbed, whose fathers and mothers and sons and daughters we killed because they got in the way."

His hands were closing into fists, then opening, then closing again.

"The rat man blew the whistle on us," he added, "and now we're listed by every law enforcement department as fugitives STK."

"What does that mean?"

"Shoot to kill."

Sarah winced.

Dwayne Pederson rested his hand on her shoulders.

"There's a real good chance that you'd die with us," he remarked. "That would be a real shame."

He signaled for another boy to leave behind one of the sacks that they had been carrying.

They were gone with the same suddenness that they had appeared.

Clarice walked over to the burlap sack and glanced inside.

"Canned goods and some fruit," she said.

Their own supplies were nearly gone.

"Praise God!" Brother Nathaniel said.

Clarice surveyed the darkness of the forest around them but saw no one, and heard no sounds other than those the four of them were making.

CHAPTER 6

The days ahead—so much filled as these were with what seemed to be snapshots of hell itself—were no less terrifying or perplexing for Clarice, Sarah, Brother Thaddeus, and Brother Nathaniel as they traveled beyond the border between France and Switzerland and headed toward their destination.

What they saw along the way was civilization collapsing. This did not happen as a result of the hantavirus alone, but added to the devastation it wrought was the awakening of prejudices often buried beneath layers of gentility and political correctness but which now had surfaced with great violence.

Anti-Semitism, as Cyril Fothergill and others had correctly predicted, was on the rise. Hate crimes against Muslims had mushroomed, but then that would not have surprised any astute observer in light of the increasingly frequent declarations of Western governmental officials that steps should be taken to retaliate against the Islamic nations.

It did not help that every major Muslim leader disavowed what had happened; nor did any of the terrorist groups claim credit for the epidemic. Such denials were viewed as part of a pattern of diabolical deception by "godless heathen," a description that had begun creeping back into public and private use.

Governments were on alert, waiting with great apprehension for more traditional means of terrorism to be reasserted.

That happened just six months after the worldwide outbreak of the hantavirus.

The first attacks did not occur at airports or military installations in the West but rather, sites throughout the Middle East, specifically, Baghdad, Iraq; Amman, Jordan; Cairo, Egypt; and Teheran, Iran.

Which in turn caused a demand in those countries for retaliation.

At the United Nations, the British ambassador stood and shouted at his Iraqi counterpart, "Retaliation? If anything, the damage inflicted within the past few days is in itself payback time for what your government has participated in against the entire civilized world. I may not condone terrorism but I can understand the motivation."

Another man from the Iraqi delegation got to his feet and retorted, "When groups of what you call terrorists tried to explain, years ago, why they had to act as they did, you turned a deaf ear. But now you want us to listen more intently as your reasons are offered up like so much stinking cow dung."

Their conversation had drifted again to their destined place of sanctuary. Once a *bona fide* fortress, the estate was now the home of a wealthy French businessman who had opened it as a refuge, an act of beneficence that gained for him an unprecedented amount of respect.

"It is an astonishing building," Brother Thaddeus told Clarice and Sarah. "I have not seen another quite like it."

Rumored to have more rooms than Windsor Castle or Versailles, though no one had been known to take its exact measurements and compare properly, the fortress was like a small city self-contained within its walls.

"Word has it that the French president himself is jealous," Brother Nathaniel added. "You will be amazed."

"But the owner has opened it up to certain people as a refuge," Clarice reminded him. "I must wonder what his reasons are. The inconvenience must be considerable. And his privacy cannot any longer exist. An interesting man, I am sure. He hardly seems a frivolous sort, concerned only with the luxury of his surroundings."

She doubted that even Cyril Fothergill would have made this noble gesture.

"Are there other monks such as yourself staying at the fortress?"

"There are other monks but not at all like me. We are different, you know, though we wear the same cloth."

"What was behind the others being given sanctuary?" Clarice inquired.

"They have had some severe doctrinal disagreements with the Vatican. The owner is far from being a supporter of Catholic doctrine."

"Will you not be uncomfortable around them, knowing that they are at odds with at least some of your beliefs?"

"Undoubtedly so, but I would much rather suffer their presence than either the epidemic or the flagellants."

The little group passed village after village that had been burned down to its foundations, the former buildings standing like grotesque blackened skeletons. Bodies littered the streets, with some of the men, women, and children lingering near death, the inevitable result of the hantavirus.

Pits had been dug everywhere, but where the strength of villagers had been devastated and their numbers decimated, stacks of hay and wood and other flammable items had been hastily erected. Onto these pyres an endless number of bodies had been thrown. The remains proved to be starkly visible; crackling pyres had become little more than grisly mounds of black ash, the arms of some of the victims now frozen upward in death as they once tried to reach out beyond the searing flames for someone to pull them from that scorching holocaust but found nothing, and had to fall back into the embers.

"How I hope the Lord will take them from those flames to redemption," Clarice said softly.

"But if they were without Christ, they were without any form of redemption," Brother Thaddeus reminded her. "Ours is a faith of rules, and those who reject the Lord break the most important of these rules."

"I thought Catholics believe in purgatory."

The monk nodded. "Many do. I have increasingly become skeptical of that particular doctrine."

"And others as well?"

"Yes, others."

The roads they encountered were nearly deserted, except for occasional bodies that had fallen in ditches.

When Clarice saw a team of horses standing alone, she was dismayed.

"They will surely die of starvation if they are not released right now and fed."

Brother Nathaniel, always the more cautious of the two monks, was sympathetic but also alarmed over what could happen.

"But you must not go any closer than we are already," he told her. "You could catch the virus, getting as close as you would need to in order to release the horses. Taking that chance for a mere animal would be foolhardy."

Clarice had to agree with him.

"Those horses will stand where they are until they drop," Brother Thaddeus agreed. "We have no choice except to let it happen. Anything else would endanger all of us. And we cannot expect the Lord to honor that!"

She paused and looked at the animals for a final time.

"How beautiful!" she said.

"Or stupid," Sarah contradicted. "Horses are nowhere near as smart as some people think them to be."

"Devotion," Clarice told her. "Is there anything wrong with that?"

Sarah looked at her and shook her head.

"You are right," she acknowledged. "I am just so tired, tired of seeing death everywhere I turn, tired of—"

But the living proved far more dangerous than the dead. The group of four bypassed other villages where similar incidents as they had witnessed earlier seemed to be occurring. Not one was free of chaos.

But there would be something among all that they saw, all the rank, awful scenes that easily transcended the horror of the rest, something from which they would suffer at night for a long time to come.

The most pathetic sight of all to endure was what had been happening to the dead or dying children, so helpless as they were.

"Babies!" Sarah gasped. "Tiny babies!"

What they were seeing seemed so like the Druid sacrifices that Cyril Fothergill had discovered that both sisters fell back in amazement and horror.

"But these are not sacrifices," Brother Thaddeus observed.

"In a way they are," Clarice muttered. "A sacrifice for the benefit of the entire village, an appeasement to some god of health and life."

"I cannot see that at all," the monk disagreed.

Clarice crawled up next to him.

"Look. . ." she pointed. "There!"

She directed his attention to a woman who was holding her baby in her hands high above her head.

"I think it is likely that she is asking God to take her child quickly unto His bosom," Brother Thaddeus suggested.

"Or she could be giving him to some Druid deity," Clarice persisted. "She may be asking that his soul immediately be transferred to—"

The monk shook his head frantically.

"Heresy!" he said. "Blasphemy! These things must not be spoken of."

"I am just trying to face the truth. I find the existence of such a rite as disgusting and satanic as you do."

Sarah was sitting next to them again, having recovered from her initial shock, her attention now locked on the nightmare scene a few hundred feet ahead.

"The mother just tossed that little body over the edge," she told them, "and it was gone in an instant. How could she? How could she—?"

"There is your answer!" Brother Nathaniel exclaimed.

The mother had bowed her head and seemed to be praying with wracking sobs. Then she stepped over into the pit.

It was an answer, an answer bathed in guilt and shame

and devoid of any desire to go on living, the same flames now greedily consuming her own body.

"Only another day before we arrive at the fortress," Brother Thaddeus assured Clarice and Sarah as they sat under a large oak tree that had started as a seemingly fragile sapling more than a century before Christ was born.

Only another day....

Although in a short time they would reach their destination, the two monks and the two sisters were weary and hungry, and even another twenty-four hours would seem a burden to all.

Despite an ample supply of roadside gardens and orchards and a few other vineyards offering reasonable sustenance along the way, there had not been meat of any kind or bread either, and only ordinary water to drink.

"French soldiers are protecting the fortress," Brother Nathaniel told them. "Once we get inside, we will have no further concerns about our safety."

Clarice picked up on the way he intoned "once we get inside."

"Do you expect difficulty," she asked a bit sharply, "that is, *before* its walls surround us?"

"That is possible," he admitted.

"But of what sort?" Clarice pressed.

"Since the fortress is known to be secure," Brother Nathaniel said, "people fleeing the epidemic will try to use it as a sanctuary."

"And do to it what they did to the valley?"

That sight would never leave her, as she turned around for a moment while climbing up the side of the mountain to the monastery, turned around to glimpse men and women maddened by the prospect of catching the disease, storming through the narrow pass, killing innocent people who sought to stop them.

"No! No!" she heard a familiar voice shout. *"You bring it in here with you. Can you not see what you are doing? You*

doom everyone here!"

And then that voice stopped.

She knew the man who had spoken with such desperation, middle-aged, with a fine young wife and three bright children, all of whom would die along with him, and yet, witnessing this, she could do nothing but watch as he was stabbed once, twice, a third time by one intruder, then another.

. . .and do to it what they did to the valley?

"Something like that, yes," Brother Nathaniel replied.

"But are they so ignorant that they do not know that they can bring contamination with them?" Clarice asked.

"As you and I do also," Brother Nathaniel told her.

Clarice was aware of that but offered a difference.

"My sister and I have kept ourselves clean. We are careful about what we eat. We do not abuse our bodies in any way."

"So, the wealthy have all the odds on their side?"

"If it must be stated that way, I would have to agree."

"And so the poor, who are often dirtier, they must be sacrificed."

"That is how it will turn out, I suppose."

"And that does not grieve your very soul?" the monk asked pointedly.

"Of course it does, but it is a circumstance that will never change. If every wealthy family gave half their income to help the poor, there would still be the poor because not enough wealth is available to help them all."

They had left that large old tree and were walking along the dirt road.

"How long can the soldiers go on protecting those inside?" Sarah spoke this time, wondering if her destination were a safe one after all.

"For as long as there is the political will to do so."

That hardly established her confidence.

"Frenchman against Frenchman?" she said, incredulous.

"If that is what it takes, sadly. You see, Pope Adolfo has

been very influential in this matter."

"My father does not have much respect for that man."

Brother Nathaniel was ready to reply but Brother Thaddeus instead interrupted him.

"My dear comrade was about to say something that he would surely have regretted later."

But Brother Nathaniel would have nothing to do with silence.

"And some of us who have served the church faithfully might be inclined to agree with your father," he spoke.

Despite the other monk's stern expression, Brother Nathaniel continued.

"All these trinkets on sale, holy water, the rest of it, we are deeply offended. New money changers have taken over the temple."

"But the holy father may not be aware of all of it," Brother Thaddeus protested. "Surely if he were, he would not permit any of the excesses."

"If he knows even a little of what is going on, then should he not be ashamed of the apathy that he has manifested?"

Brother Nathaniel was no longer as shy or meek as he had seemed earlier.

"I love the church!" he declared. "I think without it there would be barbarism everywhere, that and its attendant miseries. And the Muslims would surely have the upper hand. Think of the persecution then.

"But we cannot be blind to the corruption that has set in. If we pretend there is none, or if we say that it is nothing to become anxious about, then we are giving the archenemy of our souls an open door to causing the church's utter downfall."

Brother Thaddeus turned away from him.

"I am sorry," Brother Nathaniel said. "Please, do not be angry with me for my honesty. I can only state how I feel."

"But my anger is not directed at you. It is reserved for Baldasarre Gervasio. You see, my comrade, I agree with what you have been saying. I just have not had the courage to speak out as you have done so effectively."

"What courage do I show?" Brother Nathaniel asked, honestly puzzled. "Answer me that, my dear friend. I speak this day only to an audience of three. And none of us is in a position to do anything about it."

"But you have spoken like this to the others as well."

. . .to the others as well.

None of "the others" had survived, men they had grown close to after decades of enforced communal living. Laughter, tears, countless moments of genuine spirituality, these and more had been shared.

Gone.

Their dying moments had been observed from a distance of two thousand feet.

And the sudden reaffirmation, the revisiting through memory of what had happened, as vivid as when it happened, startled the two monks afresh, and they stopped their impromptu bickering.

"It has not always been like this," Brother Thaddeus acknowledged to Clarice and Sarah. "Until a year ago, my brothers and I had the most blessed harmony that anyone could imagine."

Clarice assumed that the tragedy was what had frayed their nerves and caused them to start acting as they did.

"What changed?" Clarice asked. "You speak of a year ago. What was that all about? Can you talk about it?"

The monk was hesitant to go into any detail but then seemed to decide that telling what he knew might be beneficial.

"Baldasarre Gervasio graced the monastery with his unique presence," he said, not bothering to disguise his sarcasm.

The mention of the individual whom her father had called the rat man disturbed Sarah, who once again shed her customary equanimity and recoiled angrily.

"That terrible beast!" she objected, with a frown and cheeks that became bright red. "He nearly killed our father."

Brother Thaddeus was not startled by her reaction.

"Be thankful that your father survived," he said calmly. "Anyone else who has opposed him is buried and forgotten."

"What did he do to disturb what you once enjoyed at the monastery?" Clarice asked not unsympathetically.

"Within a month, the arguments and other signs of deterioration commenced," Brother Thaddeus said a bit evasively.

Clarice was disturbed, and curious.

"But what could this Gervasio have done while he was there?"

"He left behind a spirit of avarice. He took our vows of poverty and denial and turned them into weapons used against us."

"But why was he so successful at this?" Clarice asked.

Brother Nathaniel tightened his hands into fists as a sneering image of Baldasarre Gervasio formed in his mind.

"He is one of Lucifer's henchmen."

Brother Thaddeus took over.

"He would take one or the other of us aside and plant a seed."

"What sort of seed?" Clarice probed.

"He would talk about getting some of us going to Rome where life was so much easier. And he talked of the jewels, the gold chains, the other items in the treasury."

"What about these?"

Clarice knew a bribe when she heard of one but, apparently, Brother Thaddeus did not let it bother him unduly.

"Sometimes a pin or a pair of earrings would be sent to a family member back home as a gesture of appreciation," the monk said. "It appeared to be rather harmless, that sort of thing. None of us seriously objected. Some found it charming, even touching."

"And you were not conscious of how this could entrap you?"

"Not at first. We felt sorry for Gervasio. We thought that this was simply his way of gaining acceptance. What harm could come of it? He was such an odd little man!"

"As blatant as that?" Clarice asked, incredulous.

"Every bit as blatant as that."

It was then that his hatred for Gervasio started to grow to such an extent that it nearly consumed Brother Thaddeus.

CHAPTER 7

Brother Thaddeus knew that God loved him and would welcome him past the gates of heaven, but he was not so sure about others of God's created beings. So many seemed utterly enslaved to a long list of the filthiest habits, engaging in acts that the Scripture warned against.

That was why he became a monk, choosing isolation with a group of men with whom he could bond for the rest of his life, rather than be exposed to the corruption of the world beyond the one that they had constructed for themselves.

Brother Thaddeus was well aware of those outsiders who would sneer at him because of his bulk, sometimes slyly, thinking that he could hardly know of this but, on other occasions, simply not caring whether he did or not, as they pointed openly as he waddled past them. In this, but for the opposite reason, and with a wholly different outcome, he was not unlike Baldasarre Gervasio.

Reactions like that were not a rare or recent occurrence. He had faced these since long before he turned his future over to the church. When he was a teenager, the insensitive attitudes of other children inflicted the most anguishing of emotional wounds.

I remember each of those times, Brother Thaddeus thought. *I cannot get them out of my mind, the cruelty of young people who would moan and bewail their fate when their faces broke out with pimples and blackheads, and they felt so ashamed. Yet those very boys joined in with the rest, to point at me, to stare, to mumble their ridicule while I could do nothing but try, try so hard to endure, to survive, to want to go on living.*

"You know," he said as he walked beside Sarah, "I worried at first that God Himself would reject my service because of my appearance, that He would look at those brighter, those trimmer and more charming men who would be greater and better examples than someone like me."

"Did He ever turn His back on that service?" Sarah asked.

"Not that I can detect. But I continue to fear that rejection daily. I fear it so much that food sometimes turns to poison in my stomach as I think about it in the middle of a meal, and I wonder if this is the beginning of the end for me."

Sarah wanted to have exactly the right words for Brother Thaddeus, and prayed that she would speak as she should.

"Is it not true that much of Scripture teaches something quite wonderful about this?" she remarked.

"Yes, it *is* true that Scripture does teach much that is, as you say, quite wonderful," Brother Thaddeus acknowledged.

"I am thinking of something specific."

The monk closed his eyes at the sound of those last two words, and heard her say something else, something even more precious.

"God looks *inside* a man, and not on the outward appearance. Have you forgotten that, Brother Thaddeus?"

The monk frowned, reminded of a verse that, ironically, he once had kept close to his heart when he was a teenager fortunate enough to have been befriended by a caring old village priest who was interested in his spiritual welfare.

"Yes, He does. That is what I have tried to tell myself over the years."

And then Brother Thaddeus slipped into silence.

Both sisters tried to speak with him for some time after that, but he continued walking without acknowledging their entreaties.

From behind them someone could be heard screaming so horribly that the four travelers froze where they stood. . . .

At first that sound had been distant, like gathering storm clouds, then unmistakably closer.

Clarice and Sarah both had come to think that whoever had been screaming might show himself as someone perhaps so deranged that he would seem quite demonic, even twisted in his physical mien.

Just a man, a tall man who was so close to dying that he seemed more like a walking, bloodied corpse. . . .

He had been stumbling along a road that led from a nearby village less than two miles north. When he saw the two women and the two monks, he stopped and looked at them, their images blurry, as he fought to remain standing.

Less than a hundred feet away from them. . . .

No clothes on his upper body, and the rest of whatever he had worn now tattered, with strips of cloth missing.

No sandals.

They could see bloody sections of torn flesh on the ends of his toes, replacing what had been his toenails.

His appearance was not anywhere near what Clarice and Sarah might have expected, though the two monks seemed far less startled. After turning and seeing him for the first time, the sisters' first inclination was to hurry to the man's side and do everything they could to help him.

It was Brother Nathaniel who again stepped in to warn them.

"Stop!" he said sternly. "Look at this one. . .can you not see that he has come down with the virus?"

But Brother Thaddeus disagreed.

"Nay, my brother. I do not think that that is why he appears as he does," he remarked. "It is another calamity that has befallen this poor soul and as far as he is concerned, hardly less fatal."

They could see that he was covered with cuts, that there were open sores on his chest, his stomach, his legs, that portions of both arms near the elbows seemed to have been burned, the skin pink and loose looking.

And then Brother Thaddeus realized what had happened.

"The flagellants are back!" he exclaimed without needing to think more than an instant. "This man has been tortured by those heretical thugs!"

The monk had never before allowed himself a display of such outright contempt, one of the areas in his life that he had tried not only to conquer but to bury for all time.

Until then. . . .

Brother Thaddeus regretted that he had let his feelings show because Clarice and Sarah were taken aback by what he had told them, and also by his manner since he had seemed almost vengeful.

"We must help him," Brother Nathaniel said. "He may be dead before we reach him but that should not prevent us from—"

"But we cannot," Brother Thaddeus, interrupting, retorted. "We have to leave immediately, or we surely will be seized upon and end up looking like that poor wreck of a man. You have no idea what they are like."

The man had fallen to the ground and was trying to crawl forward to reach them, but he was near death, and possessed no strength, reduced to digging his fingers into the dirt but not moving more than a fraction of an inch.

Clarice was stirred by what seemed a cowardly response to the stranger's plight.

"Just leave him there?" she retorted disbelievingly. "Are we not supposed to be, as Christians, modern Samaritans? Do we not find ourselves *obligated* to help another human being as he obviously pleads with us to do?"

"It would be but a form of suicide," Brother Thaddeus cautioned the two sisters. "I can only imagine what perverse enjoyment those devils would get from brutalizing us."

He paused, lowering his voice as he added, "We should not remain simply to find out who is right in this matter."

Ordinarily, Clarice would have persisted. But the sight of that man and the monk's manner, bordering on an uncharacteristic outburst of panic, made her decide to trust his judgment since his survival meant theirs as well.

"What are we to do?" she asked. "How can any of us hope to live free of how that man looks, knowing what we were forced to do?"

"Hurry ahead," Brother Thaddeus replied. "There is a
turn in the road. If we get into it before they see us, they will
never know that we have been here."

"I will not do this," Clarice protested. "That man is in
misery. You cannot deny what your own eyes tell you. He is
probably dying. Do we tell God that he is unimportant and
can be left where he is, to be consumed by predators?"

She thought of what her father would do if he were in
a like situation and she could only believe that he would be
inclined to risk everything, an innate impulse to help those
desperately needing it far stronger than nearly any other.

. . .*nearly any other.*

Except one. And it was that which caused Clarice's
determination to flounder.

"Then, young woman, you will but doom us all if
you cannot be dissuaded from staying by that man's side,"
Brother Thaddeus continued, not aware of what were now
Clarice's suddenly shifting feelings.

"I think my father would—" she started to say.

Just then, she was interrupted by loud voices, angry
voices, voices that did not sound like those coming from
normal men.

"The flagellants," Brother Thaddeus remarked, his eyes
narrowing as he went over in his mind all he had learned
about them over the past few years. "They—"

How he detested their kind!

*They supposedly adopt a theology of the severest ded-
ication, he thought, and twist this into a credo that man-
dates living a life of the most complete subjugation and the
cruelest torture, torture of themselves and others. And yet
Pope Adolfo has been convinced either to ignore them in
some cases, and sing their praises in others.*

*What has happened to this church that I love? It could
bring about so much that is good in the affairs of mankind,
and yet it ends up aiding that which is evil, evil cults such
as the flagellants and evil men like Baldasarre Gervasio.*

Shaking her head, Sarah waved an arm through the air, already blanching at what she thought he was going to tell them.

"You must know who the enemy is, and in great detail, so that you realize how much of an enemy you are facing," Brother Nathaniel added nervously. "But this is not where you should listen, nor the time to do so."

She nodded, her uneasiness apparent, as she looked a final time at the man who was still pleading with her, his eyes so bloodshot that they seemed bright red even from a distance. His mouth was opening, closing, opening, closing spasmodically.

I cannot sacrifice these others for you, Sarah thought, while trying to deal with the stark shame that closed around her like some suffocating funeral shroud. *May God forgive me for turning my back on your need!*

He seemed to know what was happening. And then he did something that ripped through Sarah's emotions.

Showing a gallant spirit, the stranger smiled crookedly, and threw a kiss in her direction, making Sarah wonder what he looked like under the sweat and dirt smudges that covered his face.

"No—!" Sarah whispered. "Please do not—"

And then the man shook his head as he turned over on his back and began looking up toward the sky, while pressing his hands together in prayer, undeterred by the frenzied horde that was about to descend upon him.

"Sarah. . .*now!*" Clarice called to her.

Reluctantly she joined her sister, Brother Thaddeus, and Brother Nathaniel as they raced straight ahead, reaching the turn while the fierce and unholy sound of maddened men filled their ears, men driven by a bloodlust so pronounced that nothing else mattered to them, all while under the demonic simulacrum of Christian service.

Clarice fell, rubbing the skin off both knees. Brother Nathaniel bent down, helped her to her feet, and they continued on.

And they did not stop until they had put the better part of a mile between themselves and the flagellants.

To the flagellants, only pain mattered. Pain was the purest form of worship. . .pain was a gift offered up to a god who demanded it of the truly obedient.

And pain was best when it was self-inflicted because then it came from a willing submission to their creator.

Yet if pain had to be forcibly meted out to another, so be it. Better transitory pain in this world than eternal pain and suffering in hell.

Pain was never supposed to be pleasant. That was why it seemed so appropriate to the flagellants as a spiritually invigorating route to travel on the way to spiritual enlightenment and perfection, so contrary as it was to the cravings of the sin nature of man.

But then something happened: Sin nature took over. They came to like the pain visited upon themselves. The greater the pain, the more insatiable their need for it. And this was no less so than when it was inflicted upon others. For some, the cries of others was a recipe for their own frenzy.

They hid the perversity of their lifestyle under the cloak of religious dedication, and outwardly accepted the doctrine of "no pain, no gain" on the way to spiritual ascendancy. But since pain had always been a kind of elixir to them, they could wallow in wanton pursuit of it under the guise of accepting a key bit of flagellant dogma.

"They sound like monsters!" Sarah exclaimed, trembling. "Will we soon be free of them, or are they to haunt us, always out of sight, with only those awful voices telling us that they remain?"

The four had finally stopped to catch their breath and, at the same time, stay alert to any indication that they were being followed by what must have been a savage horde of flagellants who would surely have killed that man by then.

Satan's henchmen, Brother Thaddeus thought, his earlier suspicions having quickly become convictions. *While preaching a closer relationship with God, they are firm in the control of Satan, and end up giving their victims not a key to heaven but a hint of hell instead.*

Brother Thaddeus was aware the flagellants had been ignored altogether by the Vatican and, therefore, few in the church felt any need to find out anything about the sect.

But the monk saw how evil they had become, and he believed that knowledge was power, and any power he had against the flagellants might prove useful to him one day.

"Demons could hardly seem worse!" Clarice added, harking back to dreams she had had as a child, dreams that began after she had seen some of the representations of evil painted starkly by medieval artists.

She felt quite strange considering what once would have been an odd and unthinkable notion, that human beings could become so crazed by false ideology that they would act more and more like demented, subhuman creatures.

"Oh, they are," Brother Nathaniel assured her, "all the more because they have, in their pathetic delusion, convinced themselves that they are saints."

CHAPTER 8

A massive fortress rose up from the field, a fortress that would have pleased the most arrogant of Roman emperors. . . .

After what had seemed to the four travelers a much longer journey than it actually was, judging by the way their joints and muscles were rebelling toward the end, the appearance before them of their destination at last was overwhelming, both by virtue of its hulking size and the fact that they had actually been successful in reaching it.

Less than a mile away, its parapets poking through a wafer-thin layer of white-tinged mist. . . .

Its extended size arose from a unique circumstance that had not been duplicated in French history, for this castle was in fact a blending of three smaller ones that had once existed independent of one another but happened to have been built closer together than usual. This oddity occurred because a patriarch several centuries earlier had had the trio built as a result of his desire for each branch of the family to have its own castle, and the safety that brought, but for them to live close by one another. He took up residence in one; his son and daughter-in-law lived in the second; and later, the grown-up grandchildren would have a luxurious home of their own.

When, a century and a half later, a subsequent owner took over who did not have similar family ties, he built parapets from one castle to the other, and gave them all a common defense as one of the necessities of the times. All of this was accomplished so artfully that it was difficult for any visiting stranger to see where one castle previously had ended and the second and third began.

A monument to the longevity of physical things, Clarice thought, not so much out of criticism but because she had to recognize candidly that her own father might well have been inclined to do the same thing. *Three centuries from now, it may become only crumbled and nondescript piles of mere stone but what is more likely is that it will still be standing, which was what the builder wanted, it seemed, a legacy to excess to stand for generations to come.*

Sarah and she had no difficulty seeing the castle from the road, a structure that dwarfed even the Fothergill castle. The center part of it resting atop a small hill in an otherwise level area, the fortress seemed much like a king on a throne, looking out over land that he ruled.

"The same, rather remarkable French nobleman controls all the acreage around it, for a number of miles north, south, east, and west," Brother Thaddeus said. "What he has done amounts to quite a strange series of gestures for his type of man, I mean, all that is embodied in the fortress and the way he uses it, this from someone who is representative of one of the most self-indulgent classes on the face of the earth!"

Realizing that he was giving in to anger amid a certain degree of admiration for the owner of the fortress, the monk calmed down.

"Those who live inside are completely self-sufficient. They need have no more contact with the outside world than they wish to have."

Even the monastery from which they had come days before was not as completely autonomous as that particular fortress.

"This one is very different," Brother Thaddeus told Clarice and Sarah, "as you can see for yourselves."

And she and her sister could.

Stretching from the western to the southern end was one vineyard, from which those in the fortress produced wine as well as simple grape juice and, of course, a portion of the fruit itself was saved for consumption at meals and as snacks throughout the day. To the east were grazing cattle. To the north, they could see various other crops.

And right down the middle was a stream that was being fed by the melting snows of the French Alps.

"It is very beautiful here," Clarice acknowledged.

"But for how long?" Brother Thaddeus asked with some sympathy. "They depend upon that which is outside its walls for much of their sustenance. And never forget that they need the military to protect them."

He was not a man who favored military might as a solution to anything, the core of him definitely a pacifist.

"But can even many more soldiers than have been assigned here keep away a crazed mob bent on entry?" Clarice questioned.

"But you have been telling my sister and I that we would be safe here. . ." Sarah said, a hint of panic surfacing.

"I did not exaggerate, for it is true," Brother Thaddeus said, "as well as can be said of any place in this world, and much better than the one from whence we have just come. There we had the mountain, but desperate men can climb mountains."

"I am sorry for snapping at you like that," she quickly apologized.

"I have been trained quite thoroughly, you know, and one part of that training has been to enable me to control myself, whatever the circumstances happen to be, and now, after more than thirty years of that, I feel my once-cherished discipline slipping away, as though I am standing on some unidentified beach and have picked up a handful of sand and I am watching the grains run through my fingers." Brother Thaddeus smiled with some warmth that Sarah felt immediately.

"There have been times throughout history when civilization loses control of itself and men and women have brutally stripped away from them all the many pretensions they have been clinging to from childhood," he went on, sounding more serious than before.

"If we have a home one day, we will have a home always. If we have something to eat now, how could we not have something to eat tomorrow? If our servants have always provided for our every need until the present, why would that change for any reason?"

Sarah thought of her mother, that pale, thin face, those bony shoulders, those fragile-looking hands that had begun to tremble more and more often, and the frustration everyone felt at not being able to help her.

We could give away every bit of it, the castle, all the furnishings, the jewels, the money, every inch of the land, she told herself, *but no act of generosity, no willingness to sacrifice, no army of physicians, no amount of love and tears could put one pound of flesh back on Elizabeth Fothergill, or give her ghostly cheeks the color of vibrant health.*

Once when Elizabeth Fothergill was feeling especially poorly and could not leave her bedroom, Sarah had walked down some narrow steps put there before the so-called Dark Ages had ended, steps that led to the dungeon area of the castle, where precious jewels and other valuables were kept in one section behind heavy wooden doors that were padlocked, with only the family members knowing where the key was.

She had started sobbing.

"And yet not one shilling's worth can buy what Mother needs so desperately now."

Sarah then sank to her knees, banging her hands on the stone floor until they became bloodied around the edges.

What is the answer, Lord? she had begged. *Can we do anything else? Are You going to miraculously heal her? Clarice and I may not be able to survive without her. My sister seems so strong and yet her feelings are like mine. I know how much she, too, must be hurting when we look at Mother and see what she has become.*

Brother Thaddeus's voice brought her out of this reverie. As he spoke he looked at Clarice and Sarah as though he were a professor, not a monk, and they were his young students, students requiring patience.

"And what about the masses? The numbers of men who are healthy enough to work are dwindling."

He was starting to huff and puff a bit, and stopped talking for a moment while catching his breath.

"That means those who are able to survive the epidemic, for whatever reason, whether from immunity to it, a stronger constitution, or lack of contact with the cause of infection, can suddenly name any price they wish," Brother Thaddeus continued. "It is the landowners who now have to listen and heed what is being said by the lower classes.

"When this starts to happen, all of us should suddenly begin to see a turning of the tables, so to speak. Those who were once poor start to earn money to such an extent that they lift themselves out of poverty. But what happens, ultimately, when the epidemic passes?"

He sighed, thinking of human nature.

"Things return to normal. But what is *normal* going to be like? Will those among the wealthy who are left seek vengeance?"

"You talk of your discipline slipping away, but frankly, you do seem perfectly controlled," Sarah observed. "In fact, I have to admit to some bit of envy over how well you have been able to conduct yourself."

"Never do that, young woman, never admire such a man as I. I urge you to listen to me, for I know myself all too well," Brother Thaddeus admonished, raising his voice slightly. "If I were the master of such control, as you seem to think, then I would hardly have the lumbering body that you see."

Both sisters had to admit to themselves that they were becoming fond of the large monk, preferring his company to Brother Nathaniel who seemed given to moods of a melancholy sort.

"Sometimes he is so talkative that you wish you were someplace else," Clarice observed as they walked a dozen or so feet behind the two monks. "But at other times, he just says nothing. I wonder whatever might be troubling him."

"I wonder if Brother Nathaniel is more concerned about the future than he will confess to anyone, even to Brother Thaddeus," Sarah posed. "His faith is supposed to reassure him but he may not be allowing that to happen."

"He does not seem nearly as much at peace with himself and his life as Brother Thaddeus," Clarice agreed. "But how can we help him? He is used to helping others. But right now he himself might need help."

"Perhaps the Lord will open up an opportunity. We have to ready when that happens," Sarah added. "I hope we are; I pray that we are."

Neither could have guessed how that hope was to be fulfilled.

Safety. . . .

The tired band of four had only a small country stream to cross and then a walk through a clump of trees until they reached the front entrance of the fortress a few hundred yards beyond. No danger seemed present for the moment, and being as close as they were to their haven made them all seem unburdened for the first time in a week.

The two sisters and the two monks stood briefly and happily in the clear, cool water of that stream. The purity of it was a relief after what they had encountered on the way, from villages with fiery pits, the grim odors of death escaping, to glimpses of people stumbling around like walking corpses, their faces bloated like grotesque, overstuffed puppets.

"My feet have been hurting for some time," Sarah told the others. "This feels so good. I could stand here for a long time and never move."

Clarice nodded, smiling as she reached out and touched her sister lovingly on her familiar frail arm.

"Mine as well," she said. "I am not accustomed to the amount of walking that we have been doing."

"Nor I," Brother Nathaniel added. "I have walked from one end of the monastery to the other, and periodically down the side of the mountain, but that was only the rarest of occasions. . .that is what it has been like for years."

"Have you ever had second thoughts?" Sarah asked.

"About God, or the regime?"

"About how you serve Him."

The monk thought for only a few seconds before answering, his tone firm.

"I have not," he said. "The way I have lived is not the only way a man can serve God, of course, and others who choose another path are hardly dishonoring Him in any way, but for me, there was no choice. If I had remained out in the world, if I had not turned inward, I think I might have died, or lost my faith. I think I could not have endured the pressures there.

"Whenever I left the seminary, for a few hours or a day at a time or perhaps a week, I would enter a Europe—regardless the country, it was always the same in this regard—so completely without the most basic sense of mercy. Christ's admonitions for mercy were being disregarded by kings and commoners alike.

"Just think of that, my friends! A stranger tosses some poor fellow a coin or two and then walks on, thinking he has proven himself to be a great humanitarian. His superficiality appeals to us and without benefactors like that, many more of the poor would be dead. It may not be much but it is all that they have.

"And what has become of one of the church's primary goals? What about compassion, simple compassion that leads the church not only to feed the poor but to clothe them as well, to give them a bed instead of the cold earth on which to sleep?

"How can the poor hope that they would ever be fed properly if grand buildings are erected to show off the magnificence of their architecture while beggars plead for money or food less than a hundred feet away?"

Brother Nathaniel cleared his throat.

"I could not face that dichotomy day after day without some part of what I am collapsing. I might consider to know about it but to see it again and again, I. . .I was not strong enough, and never would be, I felt."

The memories were profound, and while he knew that becoming a monk was tantamount to running away from reality, he could not help himself.

"In the monastery, I performed a most valuable service for Christendom," Brother Nathaniel said defensively. "Cataloguing all the old scrolls and other items, helping to translate them, making copies. Without men like me and the others, much of the old records would be lost. Where would all of us be then?"

He felt inexpressibly sad then, the fruits of years of work remaining back in a building that surely had been ravaged by desperate men.

"How foolish if they have done what we suspect," he muttered. "The writings of men serving as God's scribes, providing His wisdom for the rest of us. I wonder if someday I shall return to the monastery and find nothing but dust?"

Brother Thaddeus remarked, "It may be that what we have with us is all that is left. How depressing to think about this again. What blind, awful fools!"

"I could never be a nun," Sarah said, changing the subject.

"You could never give up everything for your Savior?" Brother Thaddeus asked, with some apparent cynicism.

She resented the pedantic way the monk had spoken to her but she did not express her irritation.

"I could never convince myself that that was necessary," she said. "There are always choices in terms of how we live. Am I living for Him less if I have a castle for a home as opposed to a hovel somewhere, with cockroaches as regular companions? Does some vow of poverty in itself bring me closer to salvation?"

"A vow of poverty has nothing to do with salvation," Brother Nathaniel told her. "It has everything to do with the way we live for Him. It has to do with what we accomplish."

"So, poverty in *itself* guarantees that accomplishment, are you saying this? Poverty guarantees a far closer walk with the Lord? It is what Christ expects of every last one of us? Or have I missed something?"

"It guarantees fewer obstacles, fewer temptations."

Sarah, while weaker physically than her sister, was every bit Clarice's equal intellectually and she felt no reservations about going up against a man, in that unlikely setting, her feet being cooled in a country stream.

"Then why did you live as you do?" she asked.

"We lived very simply, my brothers and I," Brother Nathaniel told her, his eyebrows arching, "and would not have it any other way."

"All the food you could eat, all the clothes you could wear," she continued. "You always had a very strong roof over your heads, one I imagine that never leaked, from what I saw of the monastery, and I noticed that each one of you had amply comfortable beds in which to sleep."

Her lips parted in a slight smile.

"If circumstances became tight for a while—a lesser crop perhaps, water cut down or off because of a dry spell—well, is it not true that the Vatican came to the rescue eventually?"

Acting a bit triumphant, Sarah looked at Brother Nathaniel, and added, "Where was that sacrifice you seemed to be making, the poverty? According to some poor people, I suppose you might have seemed to be living like kings! What did you actually give up? Excess? Of course!"

Clarice waded into the conversation, but meekly since her sister seemed to have dominated that little debate until then.

"If you were so isolated," she interjected, "how could you have fulfilled Christ's admonition about going unto all the world and preaching the Good News?"

Though she could not have known this, that was something that the monk had not been able to ignore, something that stayed in his mind from the start.

He bit his lower lip before replying. "I do not pretend to be able to reconcile all that Scripture teaches."

"Where does it say among those holy pages that you are to live as you were doing?" Sarah asked, curious but trying hard not to appear as though she was mocking the monk's beliefs. "I would like to know."

"We are to forsake everyone for His sake. To take up the cross and follow Him wherever He sends us."

"Follow Him? Where?"

"We may not know in advance. That is the point, you know. That is where trust comes in, does it not?"

Brother Nathaniel knew that he had underestimated this young woman.

"And where foolishness lies in wait. . ." Clarice added cryptically. "A man who may be devoted to God, according to your own view, and presumably the church's, is not following Christ, however, even if he spends half a century of his life working as a businessman who brings hundreds, if not thousands of men, women, and children to salvation, and with his wife, raising up children who then go out into the world and become part of the clergy or honest businesspersons who conduct themselves according to scriptural principles.

"This man dies finally, and his passing is mourned by countless numbers of those to whom he ministered throughout the British Isles, and his eulogy is delivered by dozens of people who found that their lives were forever touched by him. Such a man has failed, you would say, would you not, Brother Nathaniel?"

She was getting close to some uncomfortable truths and Brother Nathaniel was clearly not pleased.

"He is but one example. It is not reasonable to build an argument on just a single, exceptional man."

"The rich man who was able to get through the eye of the needle?"

"Yes, he—"

"But does Scripture say that only one rich man will go on to enter the kingdom of heaven? Does that verse even suggest that it is impossible for a rich man to be as devoted to the Lord? Difficult, yes, almost impossible, but some do, we cannot doubt that; some meet the standards Jesus had in mind, and they do get through. Look at Joseph. Is he not a logical candidate? And Nicodemus, too. What about him?"

"None of us is wise enough to understand it all," the monk said lamely.

"But you believe there are no contradictions? Surely that is the unswerving reality that keeps you going, for it means only Almighty God could have accomplished such a feat."

"I believe that, yes."

"Then could it be that the choice of isolation that you made, we certainly cannot call it one of abject poverty, has *nothing* to do with the content of God's Word," Clarice speculated, "but it may have everything to do with individual men and their needs, spiritual or otherwise, even when these needs withdraw them from the very mission field into which the Lord exhorted his disciples to venture most boldly for His sake?"

She knew what she was saying but surprised that she was doing so. The library her parents had compiled for their children included a heavy assortment of writings on matters theological, but she never guessed how these would play a part in her life.

"Monks are good men, dedicated men, but men who need the quietude of their monastery life, whose own souls prosper by being detached from everyday life. They are men for whom the world beyond those thick walls is a place of temptation and distress so strong that they could never cope with it. They serve Him by denying their baser desires but that is the *only* way they do so."

"Does that make monastic life wrong?" Brother Nathaniel asked pointedly, prepared for a rebuttal that he had delivered more than once to other skeptics, every line well rehearsed and, in his view, irrefutable.

"It does not," Clarice replied, "if their motives are pure, however—"

"However what?"

"I would rather not say."

He was not going to let her go so easily.

"Then I shall say it for you. You were about to remark that becoming monks in severe isolation from the rest of the world is not wrong, if their motives are pure, *however misguided those motives might be.* Is that not it?"

"I meant no offense."

"Then we should not consider this matter further."

"I would be happy to avoid doing that."

"Fine then. The subject shall be dropped."

Sarah was sorry that she had carried the matter as far as she had. They never discussed it again.

There were twoscore strapping young but tough French Legionnaire soldiers regularly stationed along the front of the fortress, and the same number committed to standing guard at the rear of its surrounding Brobdingnagian walls.

Not everyone was aware of the existence of the haven that the huge structure represented, and those who were familiar were not in the habit of spreading attention-engendering stories, for selfishly, they wanted the structure to be there for them if ever needed in times of instability, and the less known it was, the more likely it would remain a place of safety, a destination designed for survival.

After a few seconds, Clarice did more than simply glance at the assortment of dashing young men who snapped to attention as the four of them approached the towering front gate. Since she and Sarah hardly looked glamorous by then, rather more like homeless waifs, she did not expect to be "noticed" by any man, but, apparently, the French reputation for flirtatiousness was not undeserved or exaggerated, and most of the soldiers eagerly attempted to make eye contact with one or both of the new female arrivals.

English soldiers seem bulkier, whether by virtue of muscle or fat, Clarice told herself. *The French are all so thin-faced.*

Except one that Clarice quickly noticed, a particularly well-built soldier, and she felt her palms become damp, though she could only see him by profile.

Broad shoulders, strong-looking arms, she thought, *seeing him with his jacket off. His nose is just right, neither too long nor too stubby. No beard. . .I am no lover of men with beards.*

Clarice had decided that he was extremely handsome.

How nice it would be to meet you some other time under other circumstances, she thought.

She saw Brother Thaddeus start to step out in front of them and approach the very soldier who had caught her lingering attention.

"Why him?" Clarice asked, tugging at the monk's arm.

"He is in charge."

"How can you tell?"

"By the way he swaggers," the monk whispered before addressing the apparent officer.

He walked the three or four feet to where the Frenchman was standing.

"Captain. . ." he said politely. "There is a matter that I would very much like to discuss with you. Are you free for a moment?"

As the other man faced the monk, Clarice saw him full-face, his ruddy, thick-boned cheeks, wide soft-looking lips.

And his hair! she exclaimed to herself. *So much beautiful hair on a man!*

Fine brown hair it was, though the color was so light that it seemed almost a blond shade instead.

And those eyes, she added. *They are—*

Almost an iridescent blue, a sparkle highlighting them as he extended his hand to Brother Thaddeus and smiled pleasantly.

I am making a fool of myself, but I am unable to stop looking at someone who is, after all, but a stranger.

Clarice found herself staring at his well-muscled six-foot, one-inch body, after having spent all of her formative years being introduced to various jejune English teenage boys and later, a few so-called men who seemed innately stuffy, uninspired, and cold, if not rather fey. If she ever had been bold enough to put her arms with any gusto around just one of them—which she had never done—they would have not known what to do in response, and might have been so embarrassed as to have withdrawn themselves from her sudden embrace, let alone reciprocate with their own.

Mother and Father wanted to play it safe, she thought. *They had no interest in introducing me to anyone who might turn out to be a rascal, breaking my heart. This Frenchman would never have gotten past them!*

She could not picture him being awkward around any display of emotion, whatever that emotion happened to be.

I can imagine you grabbing some fortunate young woman that you like, and, without warning, literally sweeping her off her feet, Clarice convinced herself. *I can imagine your lips touching hers, and little else ever mattering from that moment on.*

He took off his helmet as he introduced himself.

"Captain Dafoe, Louis Dafoe," he said. "How may I help you?"

"Brother Thaddeus Palmisano," the monk explained. "You are not expecting us, I know that, but let me identify my companions, and explain who we are and why we seek refuge."

As the monk introduced the others, and the Frenchman's attention quickly focused on Clarice and Sarah.

"And these are the ladies who have come with you?" Dafoe asked, his eyes sparkling as he looked them over.

"They are, sir, as well as my comrade, Brother Nathaniel here."

Dafoe took Clarice's hand and kissed it, then Sarah's and kissed it as well.

"Your father was Cyril Fothergill, I gather?" Dafoe asked. "Or have I mistaken your last name? If so, please forgive me."

"Yes. . ." Clarice replied, trembling. "You are right, Captain Dafoe."

His smile revealed white, perfectly formed teeth.

"And your grandfather was Raymond Fothergill?"

"He was."

The young captain bowed before them.

"Did you know my grandfather?" Clarice asked.

"I knew him well."

"How is that so?"

"Raymond Fothergill was responsible for saving my mother from a pack of Druids a quarter of a century ago."

"Was she pregnant at the time?" Clarice inquired.

"She was. If your grandfather had not found out what was about to happen, I would have been sacrificed to flames on a Druid wickerman altar."

"You—"

"Yes, I was the baby she was carrying then. She lived to have more, many more. I am now the oldest of seven very healthy siblings."

And the mother of Louis Dafoe was not the only French-woman helped by Raymond Fothergill.

"A brave man, you know," the young Frenchman re-marked. "He rescued many young women throughout the countryside and their unborn children after that. It was a cause with him, because he considered the murder of such helpless ones to be the worst of all sins of this world."

Dafoe seemed to be hesitating before speaking again.

"What a coincidence," Brother Thaddeus said, stunned by what he had just learned. "The three of you brought together like this."

Brother Thaddeus knew it was good that the two sisters had found someone like this French officer, but it was also important that they go inside and get settled.

"It would be pleasant if we all got together tonight per-haps or another evening soon," he spoke up discreetly. "Are you available, young man?"

"I am as available as I need to be."

As they walked past him, Louis Dafoe winked at Clarice and Sarah and both immediately blushed so brightly that their cheeks looked as though their makeup had been applied by a young child.

CHAPTER 9

"Hello!" a cheerful voice greeted them as Brother Thaddeus stepped inside after a soldier swung open the front double doors.

A man and a woman given the task of handling the daily affairs of the fortress approached them.

Brother Thaddeus started to introduce the newcomers.

"We already know about Clarice and Sarah Fothergill," the man named Rupert Ingialdr said with some cheerfulness, discreetly interrupting. "It is good to meet you as well, Brother Thaddeus, and yes, you, Brother Nathaniel."

Ingialdr redefined the word efficiency. And the woman, Felicia Chalifoux, seemed no less dedicated to making sure that nothing went wrong within the fortress.

The man is so tall, almost a giant, yet the woman short enough to qualify as a dwarf but without the usual misshapen features, Clarice thought, amused by the contrast between the two individuals.

Once properly informed about life inside the castle, Clarice, Sarah, Brother Thaddeus, and Brother Nathaniel had time to explore the interior. They could understand why it was thought to be substantial enough to serve as a kind of enclosed village, a true haven for people for whom the outside world was dangerous.

The sheer size of the interior made even the monks gasp.

"The ceilings!" Brother Nathaniel remarked. "So very high! They dwarf anything else that I have seen until now."

"There is a reason, I think," Brother Thaddeus replied, always the one to search for a reason behind anything architectural that seemed out of the ordinary.

"What can it be?"

"I think what we see means that the second floor was

originally conceived as a final place of absolute retreat, an unassailable one, I suspect. The higher it is, the builders knew, the harder to reach, of course. And the higher, I might add, the easier to defend.

"They also must have thought of what the needed quantity of food as well should be, in the event of a long siege, and I would wager that there are ample stores kept fresh at all times in attics connected to those very ceilings."

Brother Nathaniel thought that that made a great deal of sense.

"It would take huge numbers of attackers," he reasoned. "And with the epidemic decimating the continent, where is the manpower to come from? If nothing else, the number of lives lost to battles is surely plummeting."

"Think of the manpower it took to build this, and the discipline," Brother Thaddeus said, undisguised awe evident in his voice. "I wonder how the Egyptians or the Greeks or the Romans would have viewed it."

"With a great deal of respect, to be sure," Brother Nathaniel said.

The four of them met quite a few of the people staying at the fortress, refugees living there in the hope of steering clear of the hantavirus.

But the owner, the French nobleman who had opened the huge structure, was nowhere around.

"Where does he stay in the meantime?" Clarice puzzled. "If this had been his home, where does he go now? There seems to be so much mystery swirling around the man. I fail to understand his need for anonymity."

Brother Nathaniel had some ideas about that.

"I think he is in disguise," the monk offered.

"Disguise?" Brother Thaddeus spoke up. "Why would you think that? I have never heard such a theory. We know certain facts about the man. He seems real enough. What are you hinting?"

But Brother Nathaniel would not be dissuaded so easily.

"I have spoken to more than a score of the other guests.

No one has seen him, you know. No one knows his name. Is that not strange?"

"Strange, yes," Brother Thaddeus agreed. "I will grant you that, my good friend. But are the rich to be barred from harboring certain eccentricities of their own? And is it not their privilege to act as they should wish? Should it concern us so much as Christians? If a man's eccentricities are not, in any way, immoral and sinful and antibiblical, let him have them, if they seem necessary to him, if they give him innocent pleasure. In that context, is this so unusual? I mean, I know of one member of Spanish royalty who can not stand the touch of any clothes on his body. Well, you can imagine how he has decided to take care of that!"

"I know who you mean," Brother Nathaniel commented. "He says his skin has become strangely sensitive. Seems that any cloth touching it brings him instantly much pain. But how does he sleep? Standing up?"

They were sitting on the grass in what could be loosely called the backyard adjacent to the fortress but which would have been an estate of its own in England. The availability of more land in France, which was roughly four times the size of England, meant the routine acquisition of more extravagant holdings by the wealthiest of the members of the government, often square mile upon square mile in each instance, and this was not an exception.

"But he is not the only example," Brother Nathaniel continued. "What about that English chap, the one we seem to hear about from time to time? I think his name may be Selwyn, is that not right. . .Lord Nigel Selwyn? From what I understand, he used to stay alone in that castle of his ninety-five percent of the time. His only 'regular' occasion for venturing outside was to visit any circuses active in England. Can you imagine that?"

Clarice told them about Cyril Fothergill's connection with Selwyn.

"He was strange, yes," she said, "but there were reasons. And he acted courageously at a time when Father's life was in danger."

Brother Thaddeus nodded and sighed. "If Selwyn is God's instrument for our survival, our questions do seem so unimportant after all."

The others muttered agreement.

"There must be reasons for why our benefactor keeps out of sight," Brother Nathaniel added. "Perhaps he is disfigured in some way and finds it uncomfortable to have crowds of people staring at him. Whatever the case, I do think we should be concerned with the man's kindness and not worry about his identity."

Whatever the case, I do think we should be concerned with the man's kindness and not worry about his identity.

Nevertheless, Sarah continued probing the question of who their benefactor was, not knowing why she persisted other than out of simple curiosity.

Is it really so unimportant? she asked herself. *What if it is not meant for me to know the answer? What if—?*

A chill.

In the midst of this safe environment, with nearly fifty soldiers to protect everyone inside, Sarah felt a chill and that alarmed her. At first she thought that it might have come from a draft, but she decided that that was not the case.

Am I imagining it? she asked herself. *A reaction to all the strain and the horrible sights of the past few days?*

Ignoring it did not help, for the sensation remained stubbornly, first along just her spine and then throughout her body.

Who has arranged all this? And why? The official explanation given by our new friends is one thing. But is there more to it?

She wondered why she felt as she did.

If someone has perpetuated kindness, mercy, and gentleness, she wondered, *is he not of God?*

Sarah was in bed but she could not sleep. She had been tired but rest would not come. The time must have been just before midnight, she sensed, but still there had been no relief, her thoughts continuing in their unsettled state, her nerves tense.

She decided to get out of bed and explore the fortress, hoping that she would become more tired as a result. There was no concern about awakening Clarice since, surprisingly, they had been given separate rooms but were warned that that might have to change. The number of those seeking a safe haven was growing by the week.

Fresh air. . . .

She decided that that was what would calm her down. The fortress may have been reassuring but it was also overwhelming, a great mass with her in the middle of it, and she needed to get out, however briefly.

Sarah walked down the hallway and stood before the front entrance, then turned briefly and glanced behind her.

Scores of people.

Even such a mammoth building had to run out of space eventually.

What will happen when crowds journey here and are beating at the door?

She managed to swing open the oversized doors and stepped outside. Half of the soldiers were asleep, the other half on duty.

Standing ahead of her, his head bowed as he leaned against his long-bladed sword, was Louis Dafoe.

"Are you resting?" she asked as she approached.

He did not seem startled.

"No, I am not," he replied. "Actually, I was praying."

She was happy to hear that.

"Are you a Christian?"

"That I am. And I wonder how anybody who has not found spiritual answers in whatever form can hope to get through this nightmare. If their bodies are not destroyed from the epidemic, what then, about their minds?"

"How bad is it elsewhere? Do you know?"

Sarah was anxious to find out, to get some idea of what

travel across France to Cherbourg might be like.

"I do," Dafoe acknowledged. "The number of people dead to date may have reached at least two million."

"Two million!" Sarah exclaimed, jolted by that figure, never imagining that it would have been more than a few hundred thousand.

"There is no way to stop it. I wonder if anyone who comes down with it *can* survive. I have not heard of any cases. But the dead and the dying are only part of what is going on around us, you know, as close to here as ten miles. And not just those pits of fire in the center of every village I have seen for the past several weeks."

She wanted to know. Having seen what she herself had already, she could not imagine what would have made it worse.

"What else? The flagellants? Have their movements become widespread again after hundreds of years? Or are they in just a few places?"

"Those devils. . ." he muttered. "I have had to kill several of them."

"Kill? Why?"

"Because a group of seven of them were savagely attacking a man and his wife and their teenaged son."

"But why?" Sarah asked. "What would make them do something so abominable? What could be the cause of it?"

"Jews. Their three victims were Jews. They were calling their victims, 'Christ-killers,' claiming that they were God's avenging angels."

"But were you able to save that family?"

"No," he told her. "I did not save any of them."

"Too late?"

"Yes, too late, by the time my men and I happened upon the scene. We dispatched the flagellants but not as many as I would have liked. Three were left. They fled into the woods. And then I had to put that family of three out of its misery."

"You killed them as well?"

"We had no choice. They could not have been saved. But what agony! I could not see them spending another hour like that."

He could not forget what the father had told him.

"My wife first," the man said. "Give them relief now, please."

So Dafoe killed the woman and their child before returning to him.

"Bless you. . ." he whispered. "Bless you for sending the pain away."

Dafoe raised his sword above the man's neck, and brought it down hard in a single merciless motion.

"I'm sorry. . ." he said as he saw Sarah's expression.

"I asked you to tell me," she replied.

"But it is so gruesome. I should not have upset you."

Young Captain Dafoe saw that Sarah was not wearing clothes heavy enough to fend off the night chill.

"Take my jacket," he said as he started to unbutton it.

"Then you will be cold."

"I have more clothes underneath than you likely do."

The remark was entirely innocent but Sarah blushed as he spoke.

"Your cheeks," he said, teasing her a bit. "They seem to be warming up already. When you came out here, they were so pale and now there is more color in them."

"You are married, of course," Sarah said with her usual directness.

"No, I am not. Are you?"

She shook her head.

"You are a very pretty young woman. If not married, engaged, I am sure."

Sarah looked older than she was but she did not tell him her age.

"Not even that," she said. "I have no one in my life at present."

That was truthful enough.

"I have heard that there are plenty of single men in

England," he said.

"You have heard correctly."

"Then I cannot understand why it is that Sarah Fothergill has not been swept off her feet long before now."

"There are plenty of single men, yes, plenty of *old* single men."

"I see. What a shame."

"But I was happy before the epidemic struck. And so was my sister."

Dafoe seemed dubious.

"Can any one of us be truly happy without a mate?" he pondered. "Is this not a contradiction?"

"To what?" Sarah asked.

"To God's will, as I understand it, as the priests teach it."

"God wills that all be married?"

"I think so. When we do not heed Him, we fall into lives that end up being miserable, for us and those who must associate with us."

"There are no happy single people? As I told you, Clarice and I were very happy before the world turned crazy."

"I am speaking for myself now," Dafoe said as he tapped his chest. "I covet marriage. I covet being a father. But I have not met anyone with whom I would want to spend my life."

"How is it that all the women you have met have displeased you?"

"It is not that they displease me at all," he said as he shook his head. "Most are sweet, very feminine, very attractive. They just do not touch my soul."

Sarah closed her eyes and repeated those words to herself.

"That is beautiful," she told him, fastening her gaze on his striking features.

"It is the way I have felt ever since I started noticing women."

"When was that? At the age of ten?"

Sarah was speaking humorously, and Dafoe responded in kind.

"Two years before that, I think," he told her, trying to keep a straight face, and only barely managing to do so.

"Really?" she replied, assuming that he was serious.

The young captain started laughing.

And Sarah joined in. Impulsively she put her right arm around him, then withdrew it just as quickly.

"I-I'm sorry. . ." she mumbled.

But Dafoe had not minded.

"Why feel sorry?"

"That was awfully forward of me."

"Am I offended?"

He had to admit to himself that he found her discomfort in all its innocence rather charming.

"Are you?" she asked.

"Not at all. Besides, anyone who chooses to use me as an example of restraint is misguided."

"Have you been known to do the same thing, Captain?"

Dafoe pretended to be puzzled by the question.

"Put my arm around a woman the first few minutes I spend with her?"

Sarah was unaware of his little charade.

"Yes, that."

"I have. And more."

"More?"

"Yes."

He leaned over and kissed her on the lips.

"You'll excuse me, I have to stand guard now," Dafoe said, rising to his feet reluctantly. "Perhaps we could spend more time together later this week."

"I would like that," Sarah replied.

"Later then," he said brightly as he hurried to the western end of the wall to relieve another soldier.

"Later, Captain," she whispered.

And then Sarah walked slowly back to her room, changed her clothes, and slipped into bed, sleeping well the rest of the night, but this had a great deal to do with her ensuing dream, that of a dashing young captain, his dark blond hair stirred by a passing breeze, his wide lips pressed gently and with some momentary passion against her own.

The six-part adventure concludes next month...

ROGER ELWOOD'S
WITHOUT THE DAWN
Part 6
Bright Phoenix

Granted sanctuary inside a magnificent but mysterious French fortress, Sarah and Clarice feel safe at last from the threat of epidemic.

But what happens when that security becomes an illusion...when those loved are lost...when tomorrow arrives without the dawn? What happens when the presence of God has been denied?

Who will survive to rise like a phoenix from the ashes, and fly again in the light?

Don't miss the final part of this riveting six-part adventure!
